Running Wild

Patricia Leitch started riding when a friend persuaded her to go on a pony trekking holiday – and by the following summer she had her own Highland pony, Kirsty. She wrote her first book shortly after this and writing is now her full-time occupation, but she has also done all sorts of different jobs, including being a riding-school instructor, groom, teacher and librarian. She lives in Renfrewshire, Scotland, with a bearded collie called Meg.

The 'Jinny' series

For Love of a Horse
A Devil to Ride
The Summer Riders
Night of the Red Horse
Gallop to the Hills
Horse in a Million
The Magic Pony
Ride Like the Wind
Chestnut Gold
Jump for the Moon
Horse of Fire

Patricia Leitch

Running Wild

ARMADA

Running Wild was first published in Armada in 1988
This impression 1990

Armada is an imprint of the Children's Division,
part of the Harper Collins Publishing Group,
8 Grafton Street, London W1X 3LA

Printed and bound in Great Britain by
William Collins Sons & Co. Ltd, Glasgow

CHAPTER ONE

'No!' screamed Jinny Manders, waving her arms as she ran at full pelt towards Shantih's field. 'No! Stop it! No, Shantih! No!'

She raced desperately towards the field gate, swinging her school bag, half-blinded by her long red hair blowing across her face.

'Get back! Get back!' Jinny yelled, but she was too late. There was nothing she could do but watch as Shantih tore round the field, tossing and twisting her head, her mane storming over her hard neck and her tail held high, bannering over her muscled quarters, as her hooves daggered the soft ground and her scarlet nostrils trembled with whinnies of delight at seeing Jinny. She stopped, reared straight up, her forelegs raking the sky, then she touched down and charged full gallop at the gate.

Jinny clenched her teeth, dug her fingernails into the palms of her hands and watched mesmerized as Shantih rose over the gate in a high soaring arc, landed and came galloping straight towards her. Within inches of Jinny she splayed to a dead halt and pushed at Jinny's arm, rubbing her head against Jinny's shoulder.

'But you shouldn't, you mustn't do it. Jumping out!' Jinny raged, but although she tried to sound furious she had thrown her arms round Shantih's neck, pressed her face into the pungent, sweet smell of Arab horse, and laid her cheek against Shantih's silken mane.

For how could anyone tell off a horse who jumped a five-barred gate because she was so pleased to see you; who was so beautiful she made your heart ache; whose eyes were deep dark pools of magic and whose muzzle was softer than velvet?

'Jinny Manders,' Jinny warned herself. 'Stop it! Stop it now. She only jumps out because she's bored; because Mike got away from school earlier than you and has taken Bramble home.'

Jinny swung her school bag over her shoulder, grasped Shantih's forelock and marched her back into the field.

Jinny was fourteen years old. Mike, her younger brother, was eleven. They lived in Finmory House in the northwest of Scotland. It was a four-square, stone house that stood in its own grounds looking down to jaws of black rock that framed the sea dazzle of Finmory Bay. Behind it was the rocky height of Finmory Beag, then reach upon reach of moorland and beyond the moors the far, humpbacked range of mountains.

Every school day Jinny and Mike rode into Glenbost – their nearest village – Jinny on Shantih, her chestnut Arab mare whom she had rescued from a cruel circus three years before, and Mike on Bramble, a black Highland gelding borrowed from Miss Tuke's trekking centre but now more or less totally adopted by the Manders. Petra, their sixteen year old sister, went as a weekly boarder to Duniver Grammar while Mike and Jinny caught a ramshackle school bus to Inverburgh Comprehensive. Which was just as well, Jinny often thought. She couldn't imagine Petra fighting her way into Glenbost through a winter gale. Petra liked talcum powder, women's magazines and sitting in front of her mirror messing about with her face. She was going to be a music teacher when she left school and most of the time Jinny could not stand her.

'That's the third time you've jumped out,' Jinny told Shantih as she brushed her down. 'I'm telling you they'll stop us using this field and then where will we be? Dad

6

will make me sell you. He'll say you're dangerous and costing so much to keep. That's what he'll say.'

Shantih jumped away from the prickling of the dandy brush.

'Get up with you,' warned Jinny, meaning it, as Shantih's hoof narrowly missed her foot. 'Settle your idiot self.'

Jinny tacked Shantih up, organized school bag and hard hat, and led her out of the field. Prancing at Jinny's side, Shantih sent clarion bursts of noise whinnying over the moorland, over the scattered crofts, the cluster of holiday cottages, the garage surrounded by its graveyard of rusting cars, the village school, Mrs Simpson's sell-everything shop and the little church clutched tightly to the hillside beyond Mrs Simpson's premises.

Jinny tugged the gate shut and, knowing that when Shantih was in a mood like this she would never stand still for her to mount, she sprang into the saddle, wriggling upright as Shantih cantered up the village street.

As they passed Mrs Simpson's shop the door was thrown open. Mrs Simpson burst out and raged down upon Jinny.

'Jinny Manders,' she shouted. 'Come you back here and be listening to me. I saw it all. That wild beast fleeing over the gate as though the devil himself were at its heels.'

'Can't stop,' yelled Jinny, making no attempt to check Shantih.

'It's your father I'll be stopping then and having a word with him. Or the police themselves. That beast is a danger to us all and we will not be having it.'

Mrs Simpson's words were shouted after Jinny as she cantered round the bend of the road.

Once out of Mrs Simpson's sight Jinny sat down hard in the saddle, brought Shantih to a trot and then to a jerky, unbalanced walk.

'Enough of it,' she said crossly, pushing Shantih into her bit, playing her fingers on the reins until she felt Shantih relax and start to pay attention.

'It was,' Jinny thought, 'most unfortunate that the second time Shantih had jumped out of her field she had almost landed on top of Mrs Simpson's daughter-in-law who was pushing out her new baby. Even when Jinny had pointed out the fact that Shantih had completely missed the pram and no one had been hurt, Mrs Simpson had still clung doggedly to the fact that Shantih jumping out of her field was a danger to the whole community.

'You'd think you were going round kicking people,' Jinny told Shantih. 'Or tearing them to pieces with your teeth.'

But Jinny really knew that it was serious. If Shantih started jumping out of the field when she felt like it anything could happen. She could be hit by a car or gallop on to the moors, fall and break a leg or sink into one of the moor's treacherous bogs and literally never be seen again.

'It's your own fault,' Mike had told Jinny. 'Feeding her up as if she was a racehorse. All those oats. She's ready to burst out of her skin. Wait till Dad gets the bill from Mr MacKenzie. He'll splatter you.'

Jinny knew it was true but she could not bear the thought of Shantih losing condition over the winter.

'True,' she thought, knowing that if she cut down Shantih's feed she would soon stop jumping out. 'But not the whole truth.'

The whole truth was that Jinny wanted Shantih to be the way she was, so that a touch of her leg sent Shantih into a gallop; so that she cleared the stone walls on the moors as if they were nothing; was able to trot on effortlessly, taking joy in her own strength.

A tourist car speeding towards them sent Shantih into

8

a sudden explosion of bucking, leaping from the road on to the sheep-cropped grass at its verge.

'Shall we?' demanded Shantih, clinking her bit, dancing her forefeet.

The moor stretched before them in a glory of freedom. It was Friday night. Homework could wait until the weekend.

'Why not?' agreed Jinny and felt her horse light up beneath her and with a plunging rear break into a gallop.

Sitting neat and tight in the saddle, Jinny gave Shantih her head. She felt the wind blow back her hair and whip tears from her eyes as she pressed her knuckles against Shantih's hard neck and urged her on to greater speed.

When at last Jinny slowed Shantih down they had reached a rocky headland and Jinny could stare out over oceans of moorland. To Jinny's left was a breath of smoke rising from the hidden chimneys of Finmory House, and in front of her the glittering brilliance of the sea.

Jinny jumped down from Shantih, not because Shantih was the least out of breath but because her book said that was the right thing to do when you had been galloping.

'You're as fit as a racehorse,' Jinny told her. 'That's why you jump out. That's why you're so daft. You're too bloomin' fit. We need something to happen. A challenge. That's what we need, not cutting down your oats.'

For this was how Jinny loved Shantih – hard and fit and full of galloping.

'We need something to happen,' Jinny repeated, holding out her hand so that Shantih could lip over her palm. 'Something you can win to show them all.'

Jinny looked back towards Glenbost, thinking hard about not thinking about Mrs Simpson. She gazed over the familiar moorland, the quarry, Mr MacKenzie's sheep folds, his small herd of Shetland mares and foals, and Craigvaar, the Burnleys' posh, whitewashed house standing in its manicured garden and the glint of the burn rushing through the heather.

Jinny's gaze jumped back to the Burnleys' house. One of the loosebox doors in the stable yard was standing open.

'Prowlers,' thought Jinny, wondering if she should go down and shut it. The Burnleys lived in Sussex and only used their house in Scotland as a holiday home. Clare Burnley, who was about nineteen and seemed to spend her days doing secretarial courses or going to fancy cookery classes, usually came up with her parents, bringing her expensive horses up with her so she was sure to win everything at the local show. She was not Jinny's favourite person.

As Jinny watched a light was switched on in the kitchen.

'They must be here,' Jinny thought. 'Very early for the Burnleys. Wonder what horses she's brought with her this time? Might be one I haven't seen before . . . Wouldn't harm just to look, just to ride past and look,' and Jinny mounted Shantih and began to ride towards Craigvaar.

'Only to see the horses,' she assured Shantih. '*Not* to see that Clare Burnley.'

The moorland around Craigvaar was flat, sheep-nibbled grass with grey outcrops of rock. Jinny trotted Shantih to the white-painted fence that surrounded the garden, stable yard and paddock. Although the loosebox door was standing open there was no sign of life.

Halting Shantih Jinny stood up in her stirrups to get a better look. She caught a glimpse of a woman in the lighted kitchen but it wasn't Clare or Mrs Burnley, perhaps Mrs Grant who cleaned for the Burnleys.

Then, just when Jinny was about to give up and go home, there was the sound of a heavy vehicle coming along the road from Glenbost. Jinny heard it slow down as it was driven off the road and along the rough track to

Craigvaar. In minutes Clare Burnley's flashy horsebox was rumbling down the drive, past the house and on to the stable yard.

Jinny got ready to hate Clare Burnley.

'She's at it again, carting her horses all the way from the south of England. Coming up here to laugh at us. To make up for last year when Shantih beat her.'

The box stopped but it wasn't the solid, blonde-headed Clare who jumped out, but a smart wisp of a girl, wearing a tweed cap on her short dark hair, scarlet riding trousers and a waxed jacket. Jinny watched as the girl moved quickly round to the back of the box and with neat efficiency let down the ramp and led out a bay horse. He looked well over sixteen hands high, was bright bay with a thick black mane and tail and a vivid zig-zag of white down his face.

Jinny had not seen him before.

'New horse,' she whispered to Shantih, not thinking much of him. He seemed too thickset, too blocky; a horse sculpted out of heavy metal that should have been standing on a plinth in a city square.

Shantih watched with her eyes bulging, her nostrils flaring, the pointed tips of her ears touching. Then she whinnied raucously and the bay horse flung himself down the rest of the ramp dragging the girl behind him as she clung on to his halter rope. He charged across the yard to the fence, all his bulk energized into power. When he trotted, his bulk was no longer a dead, heavy weight but full of life and vitality.

'Sorry,' shouted Jinny.

'Didn't see you there,' said the girl. 'He's been crammed into that box all day, battering along motorways. Poor old fellow. You hate it, don't you, Gatsby?'

'He's super,' said Jinny.

'Not too bad. Clare went over to Germany to buy him. He's half Trackehnen.'

'Trust the bloomin' Burnleys,' said Jinny. 'What's she going to win with him?'

'Show jumping. She's brought him up here to school him over really rough going. Suppose she means this wilderness. Looks a bit dodgy to me.'

'Not for Shantih,' said Jinny. 'But we know the moors. They're only dangerous if you don't know where you're going.'

'Bet they are. Still Clare's the boss. If she wants him schooled over them that's what I do. I'm here as her groom. Kim Beckett.'

'Jinny Manders. We live over at Finmory.'

'Heard about you and your Arab,' Kim said and instantly Jinny wondered what she had heard, what Clare had told her about Shantih.

'Anyway I'd better go and get him settled. Clare and Mrs Burnley are somewhere behind me. Don't want them to catch me standing here chatting. Bye,' and with quick, neat movements Kim led Gatsby into a loosebox.

'Of course he's not a patch on you,' Jinny told Shantih as they rode towards Finmory. 'That is total and absolute and always. But he is some horse. A horse to carry a knight in armour. Or a horse like the ones on the Greek friezes. Bet you'd be faster,' and Jinny imagined racing Shantih against Gatsby over the sands of Finmory Bay with Shantih flying far ahead of the heavier horse.

'But of course,' Jinny thought, laughing at herself, 'of course we would win.'

Close to Finmory she had to stop and wait while Mr MacKenzie and two of his sons brought a flock of sheep down from the hill. They flowed, grey-fleeced, black-faced, down past Jinny, the collies fussing neurotically as they drove them on to Mr MacKenzie's farm that stood a little way down a track from Finmory.

'Has she been at it again, the old bisom?' Mr Mac-Kenzie demanded, stopping to talk to Jinny. He leant both hands on his crook, pushed his cap back from his bald head and his washed-blue eyes gimleted up at Jinny.

'Did you know,' said Jinny, realizing that Mr Mac-Kenzie meant Shantih jumping out of her field, and thinking it best to change the subject at once, 'that the Burnleys are in residence? And a super new horse. Must have cost millions.'

'Aye, I had had the word,' said Mr MacKenzie, allowing himself to be sidetracked. 'It's thinking I am that they would never be missing a million here or a million there with that Mr Burnley digging up half of Inverburgh for the government.'

'Digging up Inverburgh?'

'With the big fat contract in his pocket.'

Vaguely Jinny thought that she might have heard something somewhere about a new motorway in Inverburgh. But she didn't care. Inverburgh was just the place where they made her go to school. It was as full of rushing, faceless people and roaring killer cars as Stopton had been; Stopton the city where they had lived before Mr Manders gave up the utter hopelessness of being a probation officer and brought his family to Finmory.

The only good thing about Inverburgh was the Wilton Collection, a small museum owned by Jo Wilton who called it a sanctuary, a sanctuary for the treasures that people brought to him for safe keeping. It was a magic place. Until last summer there had also been Nell Storr's gift shop. It too had been a magic place filled with creation – carvings, silverware, weavings, embroideries, stained glass, enamels, jewellery, carved stones and many other delights. Nell had bought the pottery that Mr Manders made and Jinny's drawings and paintings. Then she had got married and gone to live in France in the Camargue. Remembering that Nell had gone was still like waking up to an ordinary morning and remembering that you were going to the dentist that afternoon.

One of Mr MacKenzie's sons shouted, his father waved his crook in acknowledgment and organized himself for motion.

'So it's right I was?' he said. 'Over the gate again?'

'Only because she saw me.'

'It is the nasty accident she'll be causing. And Mrs Simpson as fond of that grandchild of hers as if it was the white chocolate he was made of.'

'Was it my fault she pushed the pram right under Shantih?' demanded Jinny.

But Mr MacKenzie, his shell back turned against her, was already bouncing downhill, striking off with his tacketty boots from one rocky outcrop to the next, as he went after his sheep.

'You are too wild,' Jinny told Shantih, feeling cross and gritty because she knew that what Mr MacKenzie had said was true. 'We need something to use up your energy.'

Jinny rode past Finmory House and down the path to the stables. When the Manders had come to Finmory the stable buildings had been falling to pieces but now they were transformed into two boxes, two stalls and a tack room and feed house.

Jinny jumped down from Shantih as Ken Dawson came out of one of the boxes. Ken lived with the Manders, working with Mr Manders in the pottery and growing fruit and vegetables for them all. He was nineteen, tall and bony, his fair hair long to his shoulders and his eyes flecked with amber and brown lights.

'Did you see her?' he asked.

'Came back over the moors,' said Jinny. 'See who?'

'Miss Tuke. You've just missed her. She couldn't wait any longer.'

'What did she want?' Jinny demanded urgently. Whenever Miss Tuke visited unexpectedly, Jinny was always terrified that she had come to reclaim Bramble for her trekking.

'Something about a long distance ride,' said Ken, and Jinny's imagination burst into sparklers and rockets and Catherine wheels.

CHAPTER TWO

'For yoo hoo,' yelled Mike next morning, as Jinny, having heard the phone, came racing down from her bedroom at the top of the house. 'It's the Tuke.'

'Thanks,' said Jinny, dragging her hair away from her face. 'Hello,' she said into the receiver, 'it's Jinny.'

'Missed you last night,' boomed Miss Tuke. 'Bit late now but if you could manage . . .'

And Jinny's head filled with visions of a long distance ride starting that afternoon; of Miss Tuke arriving with her box in an hour's time.

'That is, if you're not doing anything this evening, Brandoch Riding Club are holding an open evening in Inverburgh. Showing a video about long distance riding competitions. Be worth seeing. If you want to come say so and I'll pick you up.'

'Oh yes please,' agreed Jinny.

'That's it then. Be ready for six sharp. Right?' and the crash of Miss Tuke depositing the receiver rang through Jinny's head.

'She was quick,' said Mike. 'Bet you she thinks they charge you by the word.'

'Expect she's busy,' and in her mind's eye Jinny pictured Miss Tuke bouncing down to her stable yard and already hoisting unwilling trekkers into the saddle.

'I'll ride Shantih now,' Jinny decided. 'Then there's no chance of being late tonight.'

Carrying her jodhpur boots in one hand and her hard hat in her other Jinny advanced through the danger zone of the kitchen.

'Creeping off?' demanded Petra.

'Creeping nowhere,' said Jinny, glaring ferociously at her sister.

Old age was doing nothing to humanize Petra. If anything she was cleaner, smarter, more wonderful than ever. Her brown hair was styled, her clothes colour-coded and her nails painted silver. Petra was elegant, without any effort, while no matter how hard Jinny tried she seemed to live in a whirlwind of Shantih, the freedom of the moors and her drawing and painting. There were always more important things to worry about than the way she looked.

Petra's question had roused their mother. 'Have you cleaned your room?' she asked, turning round from inspecting the contents of the deep freeze.

'Yes,' said Jinny. She had straightened her duvet over her bed and in Jinny's eyes that was all that was needed.

'You have not. You haven't had time,' insisted Petra.

'I *must* ride now,' stated Jinny. 'Miss Tuke has asked me to a riding club video in Inverburgh tonight. Must not be late for that so, honestly, I must ride now.'

'She hasn't cleaned her room,' said Petra to her mother. 'I know she hasn't.'

Mrs Manders surveyed her daughters. She suspected that Petra was right. To get Jinny to clean her room on a Saturday morning usually required the heavy hand treatment but the spring sun was dazzling into the kitchen and if Mrs Manders had been fourteen again the last thing she would have wanted to do would have been to stay inside and clean her bedroom. She remembered running down the suburban streets of her childhood, new sandals slapping into the paving stones, the long-vanished spring morning bright about her.

'You're not going to let her off, are you?' accused

17

Petra. 'Bedrooms cleaned on Saturday mornings. It's the new rule.'

Jinny gazed at her mother, her eyes pleading silently.

'I've just remembered,' Mrs Manders said. 'We've run out of salt. I completely forgot to get it yesterday. Were you going to ride into Glenbost?'

Jinny had been going to ride down to the sea but if shopping was the alternative to being sent back to clean her bedroom . . . Jinny thought about the state of her room – school books strewn over the table; the floor littered with her paintings and drawings; books she was reading dumped by her bed; clothes that should have been hung up in her wardrobe lying on a chair and the dust that came from nowhere to settle on her collection of china horses and the mugs that Ken had made and she had decorated; even the Red Horse that was painted on one of Jinny's walls bloomed with dust. It would take at least an hour to tidy it up.

'I'll shop,' said Jinny.

'Money in my purse. Large packet of cooking salt and if the fresh eating apples are in bring two pounds.'

'Oh you do spoil her!' exclaimed Petra. 'She just gets away with doing what she likes.'

As Jinny trotted Shantih along the road to Glenbost her sister's words echoed in her mind – 'doing what she likes.'

'What would I really like to do?' Jinny thought. 'This, really,' and she looked around at the spring morning, the winter over as if it had never been. On one side the glint and sharp sparkle of the sea; on her other side the straw desert of the moor changing to shades of growing green. The mountains looked weightless, floating between sky and moor in shades of blue-mauve and dove-grey. And Shantih, knowing it wasn't a school day, flaunting her way through the delight of the morning.

18

'What more?' thought Jinny, and wanted to say, 'Nothing more. This is enough.' But it wasn't. She wanted more. Wanted something to be looking forward to; something to aim at; something that would let people see what a superb horse Shantih was.

The sound of hoofbeats coming towards her broke into Jinny's daydreaming. It was the sound of a horse being ridden at a steady, drumming trot.

'Clare's groom,' thought Jinny and urged Shantih on towards the bend in the road. 'Perhaps I could ride over the moors with her. Could leave the shopping until afterwards.'

The bay Gatsby came into sight round the corner, the power of his shoulders carrying his arched neck and placid head, but it wasn't the neat trim, dark-haired Kim who was riding him, it was Clare Burnley herself. She was wearing a well-cut hacking jacket, breeches and leather boots. Her blonde hair curled below her hard hat and her yellow-gloved hands were heavy on the reins.

Jinny's heart somersaulted and sank. Seeing Clare actually there in front of her brought back to Jinny how much she hated her superiority and condescension. The fact that Jinny had once thought Clare the greatest only made her feel worse than ever; that she had been so stupid as to be taken in by Clare Burnley's charm.

'Sick and double sick,' thought Jinny, staring straight ahead, forcing Shantih on with her seat and legs and will.

'Jinny!' cried Clare, bringing Gatsby to a beautifully-balanced halt. 'How are we? Long time no see.' Her voice in Jinny's ears was like mouldy Gorgonzola cheese – rich and rotten. 'Heard from Kim that you'd sussed us out. Still riding the same old bod?'

Shantih had stopped dead, nostrils quivering, eyes goggling, as she investigated the strange horse. Desperately Jinny wanted to ride on; to ignore Clare; to escape from her patronizing but Shantih was like a block of wood and Jinny knew she would rear if she forced her forward.

'I must hand it to you,' continued Clare. 'You do absolute marvels coping with her. I would not have the patience.'

Jinny glared at her under her gathered brows.

'What do you think of this fellow? He's the only one I've brought with me this time. Seeing Dad will be stuck up here for a few months I thought I'd bring Gatsby and put in a bit of schooling over the moor. Honestly, the farmers round us are such a bore. You'd think the whole of Sussex belonged to them.'

Niggling with fingers and heels Jinny felt Shantih begin to relax. In another moment or two she would be able to ride her on.

'To put a hoof on their land is almost a criminal offence. I expect Kim told you I've entered Gatsby for the long distance ride. He's half Trackehnen. Of course I bought him for show jumping though I dare say he'll do pretty well for long distance. That is, considering what the standard will be up here.'

Despite herself Jinny felt her temper rising. She was furious with Shantih for forcing her to stand there and listen to Clare's boasting.

'I don't suppose you'll be entering? Too much for you both?'

'Of course I've entered. Surely you know that Arabs are the best horses for long distance.'

As she spoke Jinny felt Shantih relax, accept the bit and, listening to her rider's aids, begin to walk away from Clare.

'But honestly,' exclaimed Clare, her words lost in her own laughter, 'one will be looking forward to seeing that.'

'Done it this time, Jinny,' Jinny told herself as she

20

trotted on to Glenbost. 'You just open your mouth and lie. Nothing but lies. You know nothing about long distance riding, nothing at all. Don't even know where the ride is being held and you go and say that to Clare Burnley! You are a complete and utter fool.'

But deep down Jinny didn't think she was. Although she knew nothing about long distance riding, it sounded exactly the challenge she was looking for. She had read somewhere that Arabs were the best horses for long distance and if it needed a fit horse Shantih was fit.

'We'll show them – Clare and her carthorse,' Jinny whispered to Shantih. 'We'll show them what an Arab can do.'

Shantih flung up her head, jangling her bit in agreement and suddenly it was all quite straightforward. All Jinny had to do was to find out where the long distance ride was being held, enter it and Shantih would be the winner.

It did not seem so simple that evening when Jinny was sitting beside Miss Tuke watching the video on long distance riding.

Driving to Inverburgh in Miss Tuke's old banger of a van Jinny had done her best to bring the conversation round to the long distance ride that Clare had been talking about so she could tell Miss Tuke that she was going to enter Shantih but Miss Tuke was too concerned about the opening of the trekking season to do anything but talk about trekkers and ponies and once they had reached the hotel room where the Brandoch Riding Club were showing their video Miss Tuke was surrounded by old friends.

Jinny didn't know anyone. She sat selfconsciously upright, staring at the blank screen. Suddenly from behind her she heard a familiar voice. It was a fruity, gushing, over-ripe voice. Jinny could not stop herself glancing back to see Clare, smart in an expensive skirt and jacket, talking to a tall, balding, armyish-looking man.

'Might have known she'd be here,' Jinny thought. 'Must be the Brandoch Riding Club that are running the ride.'

As Jinny stared even harder at the screen wishing they would get a move on and start showing the video, her resolve began to weaken. Could she really ride Shantih in a long distance ride? Everyone here seemed so confident, so very horsey. Perhaps they would all be like Clare, laughing at her and, worst of all, laughing at Shantih.

A lady with bronze hair and a knitted, tubular dress and very high spiked heels stood up beside the screen, clapped her hands together and suggested there had been enough gossiping, that it was time to start.

'Hadn't seen old Binks for months,' declared Miss Tuke, settling herself beside Jinny. 'Lost one of her fellows. Navicular. Bit of a blow.'

'If you're ready?' said the tubular lady and Miss Tuke beamed forth her readiness.

They were all welcomed on behalf of the Riding Club and it was agreed to watch the video first and have all discussion afterwards. The video was switched on, brought into focus and the first blast of noise tuned into speech. Lights were switched off and they all settled down to watch.

A tweedy gentleman sitting at a desk textured with trophies told them that they were to follow the training of one horse and see it competing in The Golden Horseshoe Ride. After giving some figures about timing and distances he got up from his desk and the camera followed him out of his house, through the grounds of his estate to a stable yard where horses' heads looked out over a line of half doors. The camera tracked down the boxes passing thoroughbred heads and hunters. Then it panned in at an open door and standing in the box was a chestnut Arab.

Jinny gave a gasp of incredulous delight. The horse was a gelding, slightly heavier than Shantih but with all the

22

characteristic qualities of the full Arab – high set, silken tail; brittle concave face; his pint-pot head held high on his reaching neck. When he whickered through trumpeting nostrils, stepping forward to greet his rider, it could almost have been Shantih.

Jinny leant forward, set her elbows on her knees, her chin on her clenched fists and stared at the screen, aware of nothing except the Arab. She watched entranced as the young man prepared the Arab for the ride, schooling and lungeing on the flat, seemingly endless work on roads and over hilly ground with several long rides as it got closer to the date of the Golden Horseshoe Ride. Jinny lived the tense excitement at the start of the ride; the anxious faces as the vets checked the horses for fitness or injuries; the great variety of horses and riders competing and the vital team work put in by each competitor's helpers. But always Jinny's eyes followed the Arab and his rider, catching the glimpse of chestnut mane or shell-curved ear almost before the camera. Instantly she picked out the Arab from groups of riders walking out along rough, stony tracks or cantering freely over springy turf. The Arab won one of the top awards – a gold medal.

The video ended with a close-up of the rider and his horse and a voice-over saying, 'And surely love is another vital ingredient in the relationship of a long-distance rider and his horse.'

Lights were switched on, people stirred and chatted. The tubed lady stood up again and everyone agreed that they had enjoyed the video. Jinny sat without moving, still transfixed by the enchantment of the chestnut Arab. It could have been herself riding Shantih.

'As most of you know, our meeting tonight is to publicize our mini long distance ride in four weeks' time. By holding this meeting in Inverburgh we hoped to gather a few more followers and we certainly have had a tremendous turn-out here tonight. So I am sure that over coffee I'll be able to persuade lots of you to have a go at a very simple long distance ride.'

Still taken up in the magic of the video Jinny stood drinking her coffee and listening to Miss Tuke talking to her horsey friends.

'How about having a go on one of your Highlands?' the tubed lady asked, dropping anchor beside Miss Tuke. 'All totally informal. Very much a first for the Club. Twenty-five mile ride. Two vets to check the horses. How about it?'

Miss Tuke shook her head. 'None of them fit,' she said. 'And now the trekking is about to start I just haven't the time, me dear.'

'Pity,' said the tube lady. 'Now, who else?'

'You'll have Jinny's entry?' demanded Clare's voice, and Jinny swung round to see Clare standing close behind her. 'You did say you had entered?'

Jinny felt herself blushing as Miss Tuke, the Tube and Clare all stared at her waiting for her to reply.

'Or is this another of your crazy notions?' sneered Clare. 'Of course I didn't believe you. The very idea of entering that Arab of yours would be utterly mad. She'd burn herself out in the first hour.'

Jinny flicked back her hair and looked Clare straight in the eye.

'I'm entering now,' she said and she held out her hand for one of the entry forms which the tube lady was holding.

'You do realize that you'll need a back-up team? Someone who knows what they're about; to take over your horse at checkpoints, run him up for the vets and keep an eye on your time?'

Jinny had not realized. None of her family would want to be a back-up team. Ken was the only one who might

24

be persuaded but Jinny didn't think there was too much hope. He liked horses to be left alone to be horses not to dash around winning things for their owners.

'Clare is quite right,' agreed the tube lady. 'Have you got a helper?'

The bright dream of riding Shantih in a long distance ride began to fade. Now Clare would tell everyone what a fool she had made of herself.

'I haven't really . . .' Jinny began, desperately trying to think of some sort of excuse.

'She's got me,' said Miss Tuke. 'I'm the back-up team.'

Driving home from Inverburgh Jinny tried to thank Miss Tuke.

'I'm mad,' said Miss Tuke. 'March hares don't have a look in where I'm concerned. Cannot abide that Burnley lass. Thinks she can come up here and tell us all what to do. So it's up to you now. No fooling around. You've to start schooling that tearaway. Get her under some sort of control. She's fit enough, controlling her is your problem. She'll be off like a rocket . . .'

Jinny hugged her knees up under her chin and stared out of the van window hardly seeing people, traffic or shops as she relived the video riding Shantih.

Suddenly she recognized the street they were in. It was where Nell Storr used to have her shop. Jinny shuddered, goose-over-her-grave. She blinked back sudden tears. It wasn't fair, Nell should still be here. Someday Jinny was going to look like Nell, wearing long flowing skirts, brightly-woven shawls and her fingers bejewelled with rings.

They had almost reached what had once been Nell's shop when Jinny jerked upright.

'There's Nell!' she yelled, grabbing Miss Tuke's arm. 'Oh stop! Stop! It's Nell!'

Miss Tuke swerved her van into the kerb.

25

'Nell Storr?' she demanded. 'Here, steady on. Come back.'

But Jinny was already out of the van and racing down the street.

'Nell!' Jinny shouted. 'Nell!' But before the woman wearing a long patchwork cloak could have had any chance of hearing Jinny she had turned down a side street.

Ignoring Miss Tuke's shouted warnings Jinny ran on. She was totally certain that she had seen Nell. She spun round the corner straight into a group of youths who were standing under a street lamp drinking beer out of cans. Jinny caught one of the beer cans with her elbow and sent it spinning into the gutter. Swearing, the boy snatched at Jinny's arm but missed. Another stuck his leg out trying to trip Jinny up but she leapt clear and ran on, her heart thumping in her throat. 'Nell!' she shouted. 'Nell! It's Jinny.'

But there was no sign of the woman Jinny had seen from the van. There were no side streets which Nell could have taken. Only a blank wall on one side and tenements on the other. Jinny stopped short, defeated. She gave one last despairing shout then turned to go back. Sauntering towards her, joking and laughing with each other, came the boys Jinny had bumped into. They were stretched out in a line which reached right across the road.

Panic seized Jinny. Her instinct was to turn and run but she knew they could catch up with her in seconds.

'Coward, Jinny Manders. Coward,' she muttered to herself between her clenched teeth. She flicked back her hair and, praying that Miss Tuke would come to find her, she rode an imaginary, high-stepping Shantih towards them.

When she reached them they crushed together not letting her pass and then the boys at the end of the line closed round her and Jinny was caught.

'Here, redhead,' said one of them. 'You going to pay

for my beer?' and he pulled a strand of Jinny's long red hair.

'Get off!' said Jinny. 'You let me past. I didn't mean to spill your beer.'

'That a fact?' and he made another grab at Jinny's hair.

They moved closer to Jinny who stood half furious, half terrified, not knowing what was going to happen next.

'Hey, you lot,' said a voice. 'What's this?'

'Nell!' cried Jinny, squeaking with relief. 'It's me. Jinny.'

Pushing past the boys as if she hardly saw them, Nell threw her arms round Jinny.

'Darling,' she said. 'I hardly expected to find you here. What is happening?'

Faced with Nell's confident presence the youths, now looking little more than schoolboys, began to back off.

'Swiped my beer,' accused one of them but Nell paid no attention to him and kicking a can he ran off after the others.

'Joy to see you,' exclaimed Nell, hugging Jinny to her again. 'But whatever are you doing wandering about Inverburgh streets at night?'

'I'm with Miss Tuke,' explained Jinny. 'I saw you from the van, dashed out to catch you, only you'd gone.'

'Popped up to see the Thorpes. Lucky for you they were out.'

In her sheer delight at seeing Nell again Jinny's grin spread from ear to ear. She had almost forgotten about the boys.

'I knew it was you,' she said. 'Are you back for a holiday?'

'For a few days,' said Nell and looked at Jinny as if she intended to say more, if only Miss Tuke, space-shuttling her van down the street, had not burst upon them.

'Where the blue blistering blazes have you been?' she roared at Jinny.

'She was finding me,' said Nell.

But even the surprise appearance of Nell was not enough to calm Miss Tuke's shattered nerves. She bustled Jinny into the van while Nell was trying to tell her that she had phoned Finmory that evening and was coming out to see them on Monday.

Miss Tuke raged at Jinny all the way to Finmory. Jinny sat without saying anything. For once she had no excuses. She didn't like to think what might have happened if Nell had not arrived when she did.

'I'll phone you about the ride,' Miss Tuke had promised as she drove away, leaving Jinny standing at Finmory's front door.

Before she went in Jinny walked down to the stables to check on the horses. Bramble had finished his hay and was lying, a cuddly toy, in the straw. Shantih had still some hay left but she had heard Jinny's footsteps and was leaning over the door of her box watching for her, whickering a welcome.

'We,' Jinny told her, smoothing her mane and laying her forelock precisely down the centre of her face, 'are entering for a long distance ride. Not too official but a real ride. And you are going to be brilliant to show Clare bloomin' Burnley.'

Jinny's family and Ken were sitting round the table playing Monopoly and eating home-made butterscotch. Jinny amazed them with the news that she had seen Nell, when they were all waiting to tell her that Nell was back and coming to see them on Monday. But when she told them about the long distance ride only her mother bothered to say that it sounded interesting and was Jinny sure that it wouldn't be too much for her.

When she had made herself some supper, told Mike

that he was cheating, and talked to Kelly, Ken's grey, shaggy dog, Jinny went to bed. She climbed up the broad flight of stairs to the top corridor where the rest of the Manders had their bedrooms. At the end of the corridor was an almost vertical flight of stairs that led up to Jinny's bedroom.

The room was divided by an archway. In one half was Jinny's bed, wardrobe and dressing table and its window looked out to the horses' field and the sea. The other half of the room looked out to the moors. It had a table and a chair in it and round two of the walls Jinny had pinned up her paintings and drawings.

On one wall was a painting of the Red Horse. The mural had been there when the Manders had come to Finmory from Stopton. Last year, under the guidance of Keziah the wise woman of the tinkers, Jinny had repainted the Horse. It came charging out of the wall through a growth of blue and green branches which drooped under the weight of fleshy, white flowers.

Once Jinny had been afraid of the Horse, had thought it a nightmare creature that haunted her dreams but now she had accepted this strange, mysterious part of her life and had stopped trying to pretend that it wasn't there. Most people had no idea of this mystery but a few understood. Ken knew but for all her livingness and warmth Nell didn't. Shantih was linked with the Red Horse. So was the little statue of the Horse god which Jinny and Shantih had found buried in the ground close to an archaeological dig. And the Golden Horses that, in a vision, she had seen dancing in an underground cave, they were all part of the magic. Jo Wilton who owned the Wilton Collection in Inverburgh was at the heart of it all and the . . . Instantly Jinny's mind flashed away from another part of the mystery. She was no longer afraid of the Red Horse but she was still terrified of the dark figure of the Walker.

'I'm going to ride Shantih in a long distance ride,' she told the Horse, speaking aloud to bring back the everyday security of Miss Tuke being her helper and Clare being so utterly foul. 'Shantih will be super and then no one will mind her hopping over a gate or two. And Nell is back. Coming for tea on Monday.'

But the thought cast its shadow over Jinny for there was something that Nell had been going to say to her and then had changed her mind.

CHAPTER THREE

On Monday afternoon Jinny waited impatiently by Mrs Graham's desk. Her hands were clasped behind her back, her eyes fixed on the grubby scrap of material which Mrs Graham was holding.

'And when you are so good at art,' Mrs Graham said, 'I am totally at a loss. Sometimes I think you do it deliberately.'

'I don't mean to. Honest,' said Jinny. 'It gets so messed up because it takes me so long to sew it. It's all the times I have to unpick it.'

'I have never seen such a disgraceful sample.'

Mrs Graham continued to elaborate on the total filth of Jinny's sample of hem stitching while the noise of the school closing changed from the crash and thud and chatter of the first exit to a few hurrying footsteps.

'You should be kept in and made to do it again but living out in the wilds the way you do I can't have your parents worrying about you. Here, take it and come to see me tomorrow lunchtime.'

Jinny snatched up the despised bit of material and bolted out of the door. Tearing down to the cloakrooms she grabbed her coat and running full pelt she burst through the swing doors but she was too late. The school buses had gone. Jinny sank down on the step. She would need to wait an hour before there was a Glenbost bus leaving the bus station.

'The very night Nell's coming,' thought Jinny in disgust. 'And Shantih will be left alone in the field again. Mike

31

could have kept the bus a bit longer. Letting it go without me!'

Jinny stomped across the playground, wriggling into her coat as she went. At the school gate she lifted one of the dustbin lids and dropped her sample of hem stitching into it.

'Rubbish to rubbish,' she intoned and marched off in the direction of the bus station. Then she stopped suddenly. Why should she go and hang around the grotty bus station? She would go to the Wilton Collection and see Jo Wilton. Tell him that Nell was back. If she didn't waste time she could manage it.

Jinny hurried through the busy city streets, sidestepping, dancing her way along the crowded pavements. She passed Nell's old shop, forcing herself not to look at the window filled now with nylon baby clothes, cot covers and plastic toys.

Jinny remembered the first time Nell had taken them to see the Wilton. It seemed ages ago. Her father and Ken, Nell and herself jaunting out through the summer sunshine. People had turned to stare seeing the brightness that was about them all.

When Jinny turned into Carna Street, where the Wilton Collection was, she seemed to leave the noise and rush of the traffic far behind. The high elegant tenements and the lime trees frothed with fresh leaves created a place of peace; a seemly silence.

Some three quarters of the way down the street was the Wilton. Jinny pushed the door open. There was nobody about. Her footsteps echoed as she climbed the stone steps and walked along the echoing corridor to the door of Jo Wilton's private flat. Jinny lifted the metal knocker – a lion's head with its mane rayed around it like the sun and drummed out a rhythm on the door. She hadn't seen Jo Wilton since before Christmas. She felt fizzy with excitement waiting to tell him that Nell was back. Jinny strained to hear his steps approaching the door to welcome her in but none came.

'Might be asleep,' Jinny thought and knocked again, louder than before. As she waited the excitement died in her. Perhaps he was out. She knocked again a third time but there was still no answer.

Despondently Jinny turned away and walked back into the public part of the building. It too was almost empty. There was no one in the room where Jinny had painted the Golden Horses on the wall. Jinny stood for a moment feeling the strange magic of the room. Heavy black curtains reached down to the polished floor. There was only one display case in the room. It contained Celtic remains and, placed together in the centre of the case, two small statues. One was of Epona, the Celtic goddess of ponies and foals. Its smooth simple shape was of a woman seated sideways on a native pony, holding a single fruit in her hand. The other was of the Horse god. It had the goggle eyes, the crested neck, the delicate head and the kinked tail of the true Arab horse. Jinny, possessed by the spirit of the Red Horse, had ridden Shantih to find it and bring it safely back to the Wilton.

Jinny pressed the palms of her hands on the glass and in the space made by the tips of her forefingers and her thumbs she framed the two of them together, saw them not as two separate parts but one whole.

Then, on the instant, Jinny swung round and faced her painting of the Golden Horses. She had first seen them painted on the walls of a cave deep in the earth. The black outlines of the primitive horse shapes filled with red, orange and yellow were exactly as they had been on the cave walls. Carrying their precise detail in her mind and sketch pad Jinny had ridden from the cave to the Wilton and painted the horses on the wall. There was only one difference; in the cave the horses had been blind; in her painting Jinny had given them red eyes. Now they could see.

Standing in the security of the Wilton Jinny allowed herself to remember the Walker. The weird, black robed being who had led her into the cave where they had seen the painted horses take life from the first rays of the sun and lifting from the walls spiral upwards in a dance of light and beauty.

'Has anyone come here and seen them dance?' Jinny wondered. For to have experienced the dance was to know with total certainty that all manner of things were well; that everything was OK.

And suddenly the room was crowded with people. Jinny knew them as someone glimpsed only for a split second, sitting in a passing bus or at a lighted window, but in that moment known absolutely and completely. She knew that these people had all come to the Wilton weighed down with heavy burdens and having seen the horses had left with a new freedom, closer to the truth of things.

'I saw them dance,' said a young man tied to a bedridden father.

'They danced for me,' said a woman whose child had been killed.

'It was the horses,' said a drunken tramp.

'They danced,' said a child.

Their voices whispered in Jinny's head as she stood sharing their sufferings and joy. For a split second Jinny saw the Golden Horses breathe, tremble to escape from the two-dimensional life of the wall, and then some schoolgirls, giggling together, came into the room and the horses were no more than Jinny's painting.

Jinny went back to knock on Jo Wilton's door again just in case he might have come home but there was still no reply.

* * *

34

As every turn of the bus wheels carried her closer to Nell Jinny was filled with contentment. She sat with a smile on her face thinking about the Golden Horses. Perhaps it was only her imagination that had summoned up those people but she didn't think so. They had seen the magic dance and some breath of its healing had stayed in the room. Had the Walker known this would happen? The question was in Jinny's mind of its own accord and instantly she thrust it away. Never, ever, did she want to have anything more to do with the Walker; not ever again.

Shantih was standing at the gate waiting for Jinny. When she saw her she swung round and jumping from a standstill she was over the gate and in two galloping strides was beside Jinny, her head pushing at Jinny's arm.

'Idiot,' cried Jinny. 'I've told you. You mustn't,' but her voice was soft with love.

She looked round quickly in case anyone had seen Shantih jumping the gate but there was no one in sight. Mrs Simpson's shop door remained closed. Jinny grasped Shantih's wisp of forelock and took her back into the field.

'Now listen to me,' she told her severely, as she took a dandy over her and tacked up. 'If you go on jumping out someone is going to make such a fuss about you being dangerous that you'll end up being shut in this shed all day. How would you like that?'

Shantih pawed the ground impatiently, flickering her ears at the sound of Jinny's voice. She only wanted to go home to Finmory, home to Bramble and the feed that she knew would be waiting for her.

Once through the village Jinny settled Shantih into a steady trot. 'Nell will be there,' she thought, and it was like riding home to a roaring coal fire on a winter's night. 'She'll have seen the white horses of the Carmargue. Have photographs of them. Maybe even bought one.

35

Perhaps she is here to ask me to go to France with her and help her to school it.'

And Jinny remembered a poem she had read by Roy Campbell: 'Long streaming manes and arching necks, they show their kinship to their sisters of the sea.'

'But I couldn't go,' thought Jinny. 'Have to start getting you super fit for the long distance ride,' and she clapped Shantih's hard neck. 'You will be terrific. Be nothing to you,' and Jinny's mouth stretched into a grin. They would show Clare Burnley.

When Jinny had finished bedding down Shantih she leant over the box door for a second; aware of Bramble tearing at his hay net in the next box; Shantih lipping delicately through her feed, searching for every last grain of oats before she condescended to eat the pony nuts; savouring the delight of Nell only a few minutes away.

A ray of light shone into the dimness of the stable, dust motes danced in the beam. The dance of the Golden Horses.

As Jinny walked up to the house she was thinking about Jo Wilton, wishing he had been in so that she could have told him that Nell was here. Or perhaps he knew already. It was even possible that he might have come to Finmory with Nell, for it was strange that he had been out. The first time Nell had taken them to the Wilton she had said that Jo must be about ninety, though he had never seemed as old as that to Jinny. He was a small man, with thick grey hair and a gentle wisdom about him. When Jinny had taken the statue of the Horse god to the Wilton he had promised to keep it safe, to keep it always with Epona.

'I should have been back to see him before this,' Jinny thought guiltily. Then, shaking the thought from her head, she raced up the path to where Nell was waiting for her.

Jinny pulled off her wellies and ran through to the front room. Nell's patchwork cloak was hanging in the hall. She was truly there.

Her father and mother, Ken, Mike and Nell were all sitting round the fire chatting. Nell jumped up and threw her arms round Jinny.

'Wherever have you been?' asked her mother. 'Were you in detention?'

'Did Shantih jump out?' demanded Mike.

'No, to you all,' said Jinny. 'I missed the bus.'

'Tried to keep it,' said Mike. 'But he wouldn't wait any longer.'

'Anyway, it doesn't matter,' said Jinny, sitting down on the edge of Nell's chair. 'I went to the Wilton. I thought I could tell Jo Wilton you were here but he wasn't in.'

Jinny felt the silence that followed her words. As if they had all caught their breath at the same moment. Her mother got up suddenly and began to arrange the dirty cups on the trolley. Nell looked at Jinny with a straight gaze and Jinny remembered how there was something Nell had been going to say on Saturday night; that she had stopped herself saying.

'Do you want a cup?' her mother asked.

'Tell her,' said Ken, as Nell put her hand on Jinny's arm.

'I'm only here for a few days,' said Nell, as Jinny's mind overflowed with horrific images of terror – Shantih to be sold, Petra run over, her mother to go to hospital with cancer.

'I came over to see Jo. He's a very old man and he hasn't been well . . .'

And almost straight away Jinny knew what Nell was going to tell her.

'I'm afraid the doctors only give him a few more days to live.'

'No,' cried Jinny. 'No! Oh no!'

CHAPTER FOUR

Nell had hired a car for the time she was staying in Inverburgh. The next afternoon she and Ken picked Jinny up after school. They were going to see Jo Wilton. He had been sent home from hospital and was staying with his son Andrew in Kilmarchan, a superior suburb on the outskirts of Inverburgh.

Jinny sat in the back of the car scowling at her own reflection in the misted glass. She still refused to come to terms with the thought of Jo Wilton's illness. How could his doctors be sure that he was going to die? How could they? Jinny could not bear the idea of the Collection without Jo Wilton as its familiar spirit and guardian.

She tried to keep her mind on Shantih and the ride. Miss Tuke had been on the phone. She had marked out the route on a large scale Ordnance Survey map and was coming over to let Jinny see it and to discuss feeding, schooling and fitness with her. Miss Tuke thought they should get the vet to sound Shantih's heart and take her pulse after she had been exercised and to give her a general checkup. It sounded like a lot of fuss to Jinny. She knew Shantih was fit. She didn't need a vet to tell her. Jinny supposed that the horses entering for the long distance ride would be more or less the same horses that had competed in the Club's cross-country event and Shantih could surpass any of them. But that didn't really matter. What mattered was doing better than Clare.

Snatches of conversation about Jo Wilton reached Jinny from the front of the car. She did her best not to listen for Jo Wilton was not going to die. Jinny was not going to think about it, not for one second. It was *not* going to happen.

They found Andrew Wilton's house without any difficulty. It was newly-built with imitation leaded windows, two tiled turrets set in the roof and mock, ticky-tacky archways over the doors and windows. It was one of about twenty houses, all pretending to be Scottish baronial mansions but each standing in a tiny garden surrounded by shaky, wickerwork fences.

'Guess what he does?' said Nell.

'Accountant?' guessed Ken.

'Got it in one,' said Nell, and they both laughed.

But Jinny couldn't see that there was anything to laugh at. She thought it must be terrible for Jo Wilton to be living in a false, imagey place like this when he had lived in the reality of the Wilton. She kept having to swallow hard. Her mouth was dry and the surface of her mind filled with foolish, polite words that she hoped would be the right thing to say, while underneath she was desolate at the very thought of having to be polite to Jo Wilton.

Andrew Wilton opened the door and greeted Nell. He was tall and broad-shouldered, good-looking in a boring way. Although he shook Ken's hand when Nell introduced them, Jinny could see the labels 'long-haired', 'layabout', 'scrounger' clicking round behind his eyes.

He nodded briefly at Jinny, his gaze slanting across her, hardly noticing her.

'Nurse says the old boy shouldn't be seeing anyone,' he told them. 'But when he heard Nell was here he insisted on getting up. We could do nothing to stop him. You'll understand if he has to go back to bed in a few minutes?'

'If he's sitting up,' Jinny thought, ignoring the rest of Andrew Wilton's words, 'he can't be too bad. Perhaps I could tell him about the people who have seen the Horses dancing. Bet he's seen them. They would dance for Jo.'

'Here we are,' Andrew Wilton said, opening a door off the hall. 'Here're your friends come to see you, Dad.'

A girl, looking about the same age as Petra, was sitting in a chair by the gas fire. When they came into the room she got up and crossed to the wheelchair, so that Jinny realized she must be the nurse. She swung the wheelchair round, away from the window, turning it to face them and in it sat the shrunken figure of Jo Wilton. He was asleep, huddled in a warm dressing gown with a silk scarf at his neck. His hair was still the thick grey thatch but the dried skin of his face was a pale liverish yellow, his cheeks sunken and his jaws clamped together.

The nurse spoke to him, tapping his face and gradually his eyes opened. He looked around him with a blankness, then focused on Nell and knew her. She went to sit beside him, bending her head to catch his whispered words.

From her seat Jinny could not make out what he was saying. Only a few stray words reached her – 'Wilton', 'road' and 'hopeless'. Within minutes his eyes were shut again.

'I'll wake him once more,' the nurse said, 'if his other friends would like to speak to him and then he must go back to bed.'

'Did you find out what you wanted to know?' Ken asked, speaking to Jo Wilton in the way he spoke to everyone, straight, direct, not wasting time on chat but talking about things that really mattered.

A slow smile wandered across Jo Wilton's face. He nodded.

'I know now,' he said. 'No keeping. Not anything.'

Jinny standing beside Ken thought that she couldn't have heard correctly. For surely Jo Wilton's whole life had been keeping things safe. That was why he had created the Wilton Collection. It was there to keep things safe – the Golden Horses, the Celtic horse gods and all

40

the other things that people had brought to the Wilton. Now Jo Wilton was dying – and having seen him Jinny knew that his doctors were right – it must surely be one of the best things he would have to think about, that his Collection would be safe for years and years; its treasures safe from harm.

The old man turned his head towards Jinny. He said her name, took her hand in his, 'You don't need to . . .' he began and then he was asleep again.

'I'll get him tucked up in bed,' said the nurse. 'Nice for him to see you all and he knew every one of you.'

Andrew Wilton opened the door for her and she pushed his father out.

A lady in a floral overall brought in coffee and biscuits. Jinny sat staring round at the bright, sharp-edged furniture and expensive ornaments. She didn't think Andrew Wilton would be the right person to take over the Wilton. He wouldn't love it the way his father had.

'We all think that when he heard the final appeal had failed that's what did it. Went downhill. Didn't want to go on living. The thought of the Wilton being demolished was too much for him at his age.'

'The what?' exclaimed Jinny, her voice blasting into the stilted conversation. 'What did you say? Who's going to demolish the Wilton?'

'You didn't know?' asked Nell. 'About the motorway?'

Dumbfounded, Jinny stared at her. Someone, somewhere, had mentioned a motorway. Mr MacKenzie? But he had never mentioned the Wilton!

'But they can't. They can't pull down the Wilton. You'd never let them do that!'

'Believe me,' said Andrew Wilton, and immediately Jinny did not, 'we have done all we can. Every possible appeal against it. In the end we were just chucking good money after bad. Spent a small fortune on lawyers' fees.'

'But you haven't done enough. Enough is when you've stopped them. They can't pull down the Wilton.'

'All Carna Street is coming down. Demolition order clapped on it all. The motorway is coming through and that is that. They aim to start any day now.'

'But not the Wilton,' said Jinny. 'Oh no.' For if the Wilton was pulled down what would happen to Epona and the Horse god? And most desperate of all, what would become of the Golden Horses? Clear in her mind's eye Jinny saw her painting with the steel jaws of the bulldozer poised to crush it into dust and rubble. It would mean that never again would anyone see the Golden Horses and be lifted up by their dance.

For a crack in time Jinny saw Shantih and the Red Horse, at first separate and then merging together to become the Walker. He stood before her as real as Ken or Nell, surrealistic in the imagey room. The Walker's eyes glowed green and luminous as he stared straight at Jinny from his gaunt face. His riot of blue-black hair fell about his shoulders. His wide, tight-lipped mouth opened and Jinny heard her name called in his whinnying speech. And then he was gone.

Jinny stared about her but nothing had changed. Nell, Ken and Andrew Wilton had seen nothing. Jinny clasped her arms round herself. The presence of the Walker had been no ordinary daydream. He had been there, in the room or inside Jinny's head – she couldn't really tell which – but more real, more vivid than the room itself. Jinny was scared. It was something over which she had no control.

'I don't care what you say,' Jinny insisted as Nell drove them home. 'There must be a way of stopping the motorway.'

Having seen Jo Wilton Jinny knew she could do nothing to help him. He was dying. But this made it even more essential to stop them pulling down the Wilton.

'Like Canute and the sea?' suggested Nell.

'Not the least bit. Of course a motorway is not like the sea. It's only people wanting more and more room for the killer cars.'

'You won't stop them,' stated Ken.

'Will,' said Jinny. 'They must not destroy the Wilton.'

Scrunched into the back seat of the car Jinny listed her plan of action in her head.

On Saturday she would get Mike to come to Inverburgh with her and they would ask people to sign a petition against the demolition of the Wilton. She would ask people to sponsor her for the long distance ride and the money would go towards saving the Wilton. Even if the rest of the houses had to be demolished surely they could leave the Wilton. And Jinny saw the museum standing securely in the middle of the motorway. She would ride Shantih into Inverburgh carrying a SAVE THE WILTON banner. A man from television would see her and ask her to appear on the news telling the whole of Scotland that the Wilton must not be demolished.

'I *must* save the Golden Horses,' she said aloud.

'Drop me at the field gate,' Jinny told Nell as they turned off the Inverburgh road and Ken remembered aloud that he had to buy stamps at the shop.

'I'm coming to see her too,' said Nell.

'Great,' said Jinny. 'But I've got to get into the field before she jumps out to me.'

As the car stopped Jinny was ready to dash out. She was over the gate and standing in the field as Shantih came high-tailing towards her, whickering through wide nostrils and lifting her hooves in a floating extended trot.

'For she is beautiful,' said Nell, finding sweets in the depths of her pockets for Shantih. 'They have a quality of

43

perfection about them. Once I was trying to tell my sister about a family – a mother and two daughters. They were all slim with straight fair hair. I was trying to make her see how special they were and she said "Like Arab horses", and that was it. Spot on.'

Shantih lipped at Nell's hand while Jinny sent up clouds of dust from the dandy.

'When are you coming over to see us?' Nell asked. 'You'd love the Camargue horses. They're tough and swaggery and real.'

'Come to France! You must be joking!' exclaimed Jinny. 'We've the long distance ride and in my few spare moments I've to save the Wilton.'

'You'd be best to concentrate on the ride,' said Nell. 'There's nothing you can do now to stop the demolition, I'm afraid. Don't upset yourself. Jo will have everything arranged. He'll have found the right places for all its contents.'

A lump choked in Jinny's throat. How could Jo Wilton have changed from the bright-eyed, gentle, wise man he had been when Jinny had seen him last, into the sick old man who only wanted to sleep?

'He is ninety-four,' said Nell, reading Jinny's thoughts.

'I know but . . .' and Jinny swallowed hard. 'Someone should have told me sooner. I don't know why I'm so stupid, never paying any attention to the things that everybody else knows about. But I am going to stop them pulling it down.'

Nell wiped her sticky hand on the grass, telling Jinny that she was longing to see her drawings so she was to hurry up and, saying goodbye to Shantih, she drove away.

'They don't rage,' Jinny told Shantih as they trotted towards Finmory. 'They just let it happen and say nothing.'

44

Shantih flickered her ears knowing from her voice that Jinny was all stirred up about something.

'You rage,' said Jinny, thinking of Shantih when she had been running wild on the moors after she had escaped from the circus van. 'That's what we all need to do, rage against things we can't bear. Don't let them happen.'

And Jinny's tears, tears for Jo Wilton and the destruction of his beloved museum, dried on her cheeks as she rode.

Jinny was about to dismount at Shantih's box, feet out of the stirrups, reins loose on Shantih's neck, when she hesitated. Suddenly she couldn't bear the thought of going into the house and having to listen to them talking about the demolition of the Wilton as if it had already happened. On an impulse she closed her legs against Shantih's sides and sent her storming on down to the sea.

When they came to the banking of sea-smoothed boulders which lay between the path and the sands, Jinny brought Shantih to a walk, letting her pick her own way through them, but when they reached the sands she shortened her reins, sat forward in the saddle and with a half rear Shantih leapt into a gallop.

The spring evening was calm in shades of grey. Gulls planed through luminous grey light sweeping over the pewter glitter of the sea. The glistening silver from the withdrawing tide stretched before Jinny to the rocks at the far end of Finmory Bay.

'Faster,' Jinny whispered. 'Faster.'

She wanted to gallop on and on, never to stop; for while she was astride Shantih she was safe. Nothing could reach her here. As Jinny shared her horse's plunging strength the thought of Jo Wilton dying, of the Golden Horses being smashed to dust and even the excitement of the long distance ride were left far behind.

Shantih, head snaked forward, neck stretched low,

thundering along the wet sands. The thought flickered in Jinny's mind that she had never known Shantih to gallop as fast as this. But she didn't care. Jinny only wanted speed and more speed, wanted Shantih to gallop faster than the spinning globe.

They had almost reached the rocks at the other side of the bay when Shantih flung herself sideways and swerved to a sudden rearing halt. Jinny, clutching mane and reins, just managed to stay on top.

'What on earth made you do that?' Jinny cried.

But Shantih was paying no attention to her rider. She was standing rigid. Her neck was arched, her ears pointed sharply forward as she stared in the direction of the rocks.

'What can you see?' Jinny demanded, trying to make out what it was that had startled Shantih.

Shantih whinnied into the grey stillness with a high pitched call, and at the same moment Jinny saw that there was someone standing by the rocks. A figure with black, windblown clothing and a jet-black mane of hair. It was the Walker.

Jinny screamed with the full pitch of her lungs. She tugged furiously on her right rein and kicked wildly with her left heel as she fought to turn Shantih.

The Walker took a slow step towards them and held out his hand.

Jinny's terror gave her strength. With all her will she struggled against Shantih. Sitting tight down in the saddle, digging both heels viciously into Shantih's sides, Jinny pushed her into a trot and then a canter; driving her on when Shantih's one desire was to be galloping back to the Walker.

Jinny clattered Shantih over the boulders, ignoring her desperate whinnying. When they reached the path that led to Finmory she urged her into a gallop again. In the stable Jinny saw to Shantih as quickly as she could, glad of Bramble's hay-chomping presence.

'Now calm yourself,' she told Shantih when her bed was set square, hay net and water bucket filled and her feed in the trough. 'There was nothing out there. Not a thing. Only shadows on the rocks.'

For a long moment Jinny hesitated by the stables, then hiding her face behind her hair she bolted for home.

'You've been a long time,' said Mrs Manders, as Jinny joined the others round the kitchen table. 'We've nearly finished.'

'If it's veggie pie can I have a huge slice?' Jinny asked, drawing her mother's attention away from her own panic.

In the evening when Nell asked to see Jinny's paintings Jinny did not take Nell up to her room where the Red Horse would be watching them. Instead she brought a selection down to Nell and endured her family's comments.

'Ah yes,' said Nell, 'I do like this one,' and she held up a watercolour of Jinny riding Shantih bareback with a riderless black horse galloping at her side. The black horse had a mane tangled and clotted with waterweed; its green eyes stared from its skeletal head. 'How much?'

'Not for sale,' stated Jinny. She hadn't meant to include the picture and tried to take it from Nell without anyone else seeing it but she was too late.

'Is this one of your nightmares?' her father asked, taking it from Nell.

'Why on earth do you paint these things?' her mother asked, as if it was something that Jinny chose to do.

Only Ken had any idea what the painting meant. The black horse was another form of the Walker.

After Nell had gone and Jinny, taking Kelly with her, had been down to the stables to say good night to the horses she remembered that she hadn't done her French homework. Mr Fisher wanted it handed in tomorrow. Jinny thought hard about Mr Fisher's special brand of sarcasm and decided that she had better get on with it.

Reluctantly she dragged her school bag upstairs to her room, sat down with her back to the Red Horse, took out her French books and, propping her head on her hands, read the first French sentence and stared hopelessly at it. Her mind wandered to Shantih, to Clare and Gatsby, and then to Jo Wilton waiting to die while the most precious thing in his life was about to be destroyed.

'I'll find a way to stop them,' Jinny swore. 'I shan't let them pull it down. They shan't destroy the Golden Horses,' and she began to decorate the edges of her jotter with drawings of the Golden Horses.

Suddenly she felt a chill creep up her spine, the hair on the back of her neck stood upright with fear. There was someone standing behind her.

Jinny sprang up, swinging round to confront the intruder, her chair crashing to the floor.

But there was no one there. Only the painting of the Red Horse seemed to glow with energy. Its yellow eyes with their red pupils were staring straight at Jinny.

CHAPTER FIVE

The basic things Jinny was to aim for in schooling Shantih for the ride were balance, free forward movement and rhythm. Miss Tuke had told Jinny this when she had come over on Wednesday evening to discuss the ride. She had pronounced Shantih as fit but had said they would need to get the vet out to check her over. She had also brought a diet sheet for Shantih, saying that she was going over to her grain merchant at the weekend, would buy the extras that Shantih needed and see Mr Manders about the money later.

Jinny had nodded, not thinking too much about what her father would say at the prospect of vet's fees and food bills. That was one thing that Clare Burnley would not have to worry about.

'Shantih's used to rough going,' Miss Tuke had said. 'All that charging around you do. Anything she meets on the ride will be nothing compared to that. What we don't want is her going off her head for the first ten miles and then total exhaustion before the end.'

'But she won't be exhausted. She likes going fast. She's best that way.'

Miss Tuke had not agreed and Jinny hadn't been in the least surprised to be told that the best thing to stop Shantih wasting her energy in bad behaviour was schooling. Riding wildly between Glenbost and Finmory was to stop as well. Jinny was to cease daydreaming and pay attention to her riding, making accurate changes from walk to trot and trot to canter. She was to use her legs and seat to keep the rhythm of the pace she was riding at and all halts were to be straight and square not a plunging fight.

'Shantih will not be happy,' Jinny had warned.

'Do you think Clare worries about Gatsby's finer feelings?' Miss Tuke had demanded and that had been final.

Just after seven the next Saturday morning Jinny was trotting schooling circles in Shantih's field. Riding at a sitting trot she was working on changing direction and pace. Shantih, her tail tucked down against the steady rain, her ears snaked back, was thinking about Bramble still in his box and, Shantih suspected, not only warm and dry but munching hay as well. Everytime they trotted towards the gate Shantih set her jaw and leant towards it.

'We've another ten minutes,' Jinny told her, pushing her on. 'Pigging off to that gate will make no difference. Now trot on with you.

'We're wasting time,' Jinny thought. 'Neither of us are concentrating. Just mucking about.'

Jinny's mind was fixed on the day ahead, of organizing Mike into Inverburgh with the sheaf of petitions she had made out the previous evening. On each sheet she had drawn four of the Golden Horses for luck. Mike had not been too keen on the idea of spending his day standing outside the Wilton petitioning but only a few weeks before Jinny had gone to watch one of his football matches, standing in the freezing cold with a handful of doting parents when she could have been riding.

'You must come,' Jinny had told him. 'You're in debt.'

Both Shantih and Bramble were still in at night so Jinny left Shantih in her box with her hay net while she went in to have her own breakfast.

A shape moved at the back door as Jinny dashed through the rain. She froze instantly. Since Tuesday night there had been no more sign of the Walker – if it had been the Walker she had seen on the beach – and the Red

Horse had been no more than a painting. Jinny had pushed the incident to the back of her mind, concentrating on the danger to the Wilton and on schooling Shantih. But now the movement, seen through the rhododendrons, flickered the black dread of the Walker before Jinny's eyes.

'I was passing by to the sheep,' said Mr MacKenzie. 'So here is your milk, and myself the milk boy.'

He regarded Jinny's dripping figure with amusement.

'Have you been getting the good of the beautiful weather?' he asked.

No matter what the weather was like Mr MacKenzie rarely wore anything other than his casing of tweed which seemed totally waterproof and sunproof. If it had not been for his Sunday black Jinny would have suspected that he had grown a tweed skin.

'Mike was telling me that you are off to Inverburgh with the petitions in your hands and then straight to No. 10 with you?'

'Good idea,' said Jinny. 'Had not thought of that.'

'If you are at the farm inside the hour it is myself will drive you to Glenbost.'

'Well . . .' said Jinny hesitating, for she knew that the temptation of a lift into the village usually meant that you had to walk back. If she took Shantih she could ride both ways.

Mike had no doubts.

'Lift it is,' he exclaimed, emerging from under the bedclothes when Jinny told him.

Three-quarters of an hour later they were both hurrying down the track to the farm.

'Glory, the horses!' Jinny exclaimed. 'Forgot them,' and she was running madly in the opposite direction before Mike had time to realize what had happened.

51

Mr MacKenzie was sitting at the wheel of his car, revving the engine when Jinny reached the yard.

'Sorry,' she gasped, tumbling into the back seat as Mike held the door open for her. 'Nearly left the horses standing in.'

Mr MacKenzie dropped them at Glenbost and drove on to Ardtallon. Twenty minutes later the bus for Inverburgh came into sight.

'I'm soaked to the skin already,' Mike moaned. 'What are we going to be like after hanging about Inverburgh all morning?'

'Day,' said Jinny, holding her arm out to stop the bus.

It was still raining when they got off the bus at Inverburgh; a steady downpour that showed no sign of stopping.

'We'll stand outside the Wilton,' said Jinny, leading the way. 'People going into the Wilton are certain to want to save it.'

'This is totally mad. You haven't a chance. A boy in my class said that the whole thing had been fixed months ago. They're almost ready to start work on the motorway.'

Jinny ignored her brother.

'When we've got enough signatures I'll take it to the Town Hall.'

'There'll be nobody there on a Saturday.'

'Bound to be someone. Town Halls don't just shut. There's always someone there in case . . .' but Jinny couldn't think exactly why.

'There's a revolution?' suggested Mike, thinking it as likely as Jinny getting any signatures on her petition on a day like this.

To begin with they stood by the Wilton but Carna Street was almost deserted. Even when they moved to the busier streets no one was interested. Most people hadn't even heard of the Wilton Collection but they had heard of the motorway and thought it a good thing, removing through traffic from the Inverburgh streets. The few people who did stop and sign their names only did so to appease Jinny's dripping intensity.

By one o'clock Jinny had twenty-three signatures and Mike eleven.

'Come on,' said Mike. 'Give up.'

'No.'

'Food then,' stated Mike.

They found a lino-floored cafe with plastic seats and ordered egg and chips and coke. When they had finished Jinny began to write more names on the petition, changing her handwriting for each signature.

'Watch it,' said Mike. 'You're not allowed to do that. It's illegal.'

'They're all people I know,' said Jinny, scribbling rapidly. 'If they were here they'd want to sign. All I'm doing is writing their names for them.'

'You don't even know that many people,' said Mike, when Jinny had filled in three sheets of the petition.

'Do.'

'Do not. You do not know Bob Geldof.'

'I know how he thinks. He wouldn't want the motorway. He'd want the Wilton to be left alone.'

Reluctantly Mike agreed to go back to the Wilton for another hour.

'The thing about being totally soaking is that you stop even knowing you're wet,' said Jinny.

'I know I'm wet. One hour and that's it.'

'OK,' agreed Jinny. 'And then the Town Hall.'

Mike groaned. 'Petra's right,' he said. 'Once you get going you are quite crazy.'

After an hour of standing in the Wilton doorway they had only eight more signatures.

'That's your lot,' said Mike as the hands of his watch touched two-thirty.

At the same moment two men and a girl came hurrying down the opposite side of the street. They were all sheltering behind a huge black umbrella held by one of the men.

Jinny dashed across to them.

'Excuse me,' she said loudly, more or less speaking to the umbrella, 'would you like to sign a petition to stop the Wilton being demolished?'

'Being hailed on my port side,' announced one of the young men and lifted up the umbrella.

'Clare!' Jinny exclaimed in dismay.

'Heavens,' said Clare. 'The ubiquitous Manders.'

Trying not to think about how she must look, Jinny repeated her request.

'I should say not,' laughed Clare. 'Can't stop. We're dashing.'

As they hurried on one of the men said something which Jinny couldn't quite hear, something about Clare's Old Man, and Jinny being on a losing wicket.

'Well, surely that's enough for you?' said Mike, when Jinny came back.

For a minute Jinny felt her spirits sink. As if a few rain-sodden sheets of mostly made-up signatures could possibly change anything. She stared bleakly up and down the road at the high stone buildings. They seemed so safe, so secure, as if nothing could ever change or harm them. She pressed the palm of her hand against the stone wall of the Wilton. How was it possible that anyone should want to come and destroy it all? She thought of the Horse god and Epona; of the Golden Horses, and felt burning tears filling her eyes. Instantly she squared her shoulders, slicked back her hair and taking Mike's sheet from him she added it to her own.

'Right,' she said. 'The Town Hall!'

When they reached the marble pillars of the Town Hall Mike looked at his watch. 'You've got half an hour,' he said. 'See you at the bus station,' and he was gone.

'Pig,' thought Jinny as she turned and pushed her way through the swing doors into the marble hallway. A broad flight of marble stairs flowed up in front of her. A large notice board directed her to the various departments. Jinny stared at it hopelessly. She had no idea where she wanted to go.

Then she saw a window marked 'Enquiries', with a bell beside it. Jinny hesitated, wondering if she should go home, give the whole thing up.

'You can't,' she told herself fiercely. 'You can't. You were chosen to bring the Golden Horses from the cave. You have the responsibility for them,' and she remembered how Shantih, after a long day's riding, had carried her through the dangers of the Inverburgh traffic to bring her drawings of the Golden Horses safely to the Wilton. Shantih hadn't given up then. She couldn't give up now.

She pressed the bell, waited, rang again and the glass window was pushed open.

'Well?' demanded a peaked cap and a wrinkled face. 'What department? Nearly all shut. It's Saturday.'

'Roads,' said Jinny, guessing wildly.

'Umph!' snorted the peaked cap as if he was put out that Jinny had chosen a department that was open. 'Second Floor. Third door on your right. Number 52. You'll need to walk. No lift, it's Saturday.'

After several cautious knocks on No. 52 Jinny tried the handle, found the door open and went in. A long empty counter faced her but there was another door at the end of the counter. Jinny knocked, heard a woman's voice telling her to come in, and opening the door found herself

55

in a tiny office where a very fat woman sat at a small desk overflowing with computer printouts.

'I've brought a petition to stop them pulling down the Wilton. You can't possibly demolish it. It's the best museum in Inverburgh.'

There was a wall mirror behind the woman. In it a skinny girl, her eyes wild, her long red hair darkened and flattened by the rain stood holding a bundle of sodden sheets of paper.

The woman's puffy face quivered before she spoke.

'I have no idea what you are talking about,' she said. 'And I cannot imagine what you are doing here but please, stop dripping over my desk.'

Jinny backed off and tried again.

'Oh, it's the motorway you're going on about,' exclaimed the woman when Jinny had finished.

'You've got to stop it,' garbled Jinny. 'No one wants it. Everyone has signed my petition.'

'As luck would have it,' said the fat woman, burrowing through her papers, 'I can tell you . . . Here it is. Now where is this museum?'

'Carna Street.'

'Demolition starts the week after next. The whole contract for the motorway was signed months ago. Went to an English firm,' and she scrabbled through her piles of paper again. 'Yes, Burnley Builders. A Mr Burnley. Close competition but he got it.'

The walls of the office flowed around Jinny like the sea. The carpeted floor began to float beneath her feet.

'What's wrong?' said the woman, as she pushed herself to her feet and came stomping round the desk.

Jinny felt her shoulders being grasped as she was guided to a chair and her head was pushed down.

'I'm OK now,' Jinny said minutes later, as she cautiously looked up. 'It's just . . .'

And it was Jo Wilton dying; the walls of the Wilton crumbling to rubble; the dance of the Golden Horses lost forever. It was the hopelessness of not being able to do anything to change it. And of all people Clare Burnley's father was to be in charge of it. He was to make money out of the destruction of the Wilton.

Suddenly Jinny wanted to be with Shantih, wanted to be riding her, safe in her strength and speed. Wanted her more than anything else in the world.

Jinny sat for a moment longer then seeing a clock on the wall realized that she must go or she would miss the bus.

'I'm sorry to have bothered you. It's not your fault but thank you.'

For a second Jinny thought of leaving the petition but knew it was useless.

'Thank you,' she said again and scuttled out of the office, hurtled down the marble staircase and out through the swing doors. She dumped the petition in the first waste bin she came to.

The bus driver was starting up the bus as Jinny jumped on.

'Near thing,' he said.

'Nearly wasn't,' agreed Jinny, thinking that to have missed the bus would have been the final straw to a truly awful day.

Mike was sitting next to a schoolfriend so Jinny was able to sit alone, closing her mind to everything except Shantih and the long distance ride.

'What happened to the petition?' Mike asked as they splodged their way back to Finmory.

'Left it,' said Jinny, but she didn't say where.

'You'll need to come to a dozen matches to pay me back for this.'

Jinny didn't reply. She knew he was right. Half a dozen

anyway but she wasn't going to argue. Not just now. Soon she would be with Shantih and that was all she cared about.

'I'll see to the horses,' Jinny said when they reached home. 'Will you heat up some soup?'

'OK,' said Mike. 'Be quick.'

'Right,' said Jinny.

She stopped at the stables hoping that someone might have brought them in but both boxes were empty.

Wind from the sea blasted in against her, sudden squalls of rain daggered into her face and frozen hands. She put her head down and battered on. Down past the hedge of the horses' field she went without looking up.

As she approached the gate she turned her back to the gale, clawed her hair away from her face, and yelled to the horses.

'Shantih! Bramble! Come, come up!'

But there was no sound of stampeding hooves, no whinnying welcome.

And then she saw that the field gate was open and the field was empty.

CHAPTER SIX

Jinny gripped the top bar of the gate, stared desperately round the field but beyond all shadow of doubt it was empty. With a sudden sinking guilt she remembered her rush to turn the forgotten horses out that morning. Had she made certain that the gate was properly shut? She couldn't remember, only the dash and hurry; Bramble tanking past Shantih in his eagerness to get into the field first. And with the thought of Bramble, his black, hairy bulk cramming at the gate, came the vivid memory of swinging the gate shut; of thinking she hadn't time to bother with the bolt. The gate must have blown open. It was her fault that Bramble and Shantih had got out.

For a moment Jinny stood frozen to the spot. Visions of Shantih galloping crazily over the moors filled her mind; of Shantih in her drum-tight fitness catching her hooves in the treacherous net of winter-petrified heather and dead bracken, crashing to the ground, struggling to get up, her shoulder strained, her back damaged or – most terrible of all – standing with a leg limp and useless, a broken leg that could mean only one thing – she would have to be shot. Jinny saw the gaudy scum-green of the moorland bogs that would suck a horse down to its death. And all her own fault.

'Don't,' Jinny shouted, breaking from her evil imaginings. 'Get help. Tell the others,' she thought, and went tearing back to Finmory.

As she ran past the dense rhododendron shrubbery Bramble's hairy face and leaf-knotted mane looked out at her.

'Bramble!' Jinny cried, and he came plodding through the rain towards her.

Jinny grabbed him, shouting abuse at him because she was so pleased to see him safe. 'Where's Shantih?' she demanded. 'Shantih! Shantih!' she yelled, but no red-gold shape came galloping to answer her call.

'Shantih! Shantih!' she yelled. 'Come up the horse. Shantih, come. Come.'

Wind howled through the bushes, wailed in from the sea but it brought no sound of hooves.

Dragging Bramble by the forelock Jinny forced him towards the house. She knew that if Shantih had heard her she would have come to her by now.

'What's up with Bramble?' Mike demanded, opening the door to Jinny's urgent hammering.

'They both got out. I didn't bolt the gate. He was in the shrubbery but Shantih's gone.'

Mrs Manders, hearing Jinny's excited voice, came to listen.

'Take Bramble back to his box,' she said firmly, cutting through Jinny's hysteria. 'See to him and while you're doing that I'll phone round and find out if anyone's seen Shantih.'

'Where did she go?' Jinny asked Bramble. 'You must have seen her,' but Bramble only stamped impatient hooves on the floor of his box demanding his feed.

No one at the farm had seen Shantih or heard her galloping past. She hadn't gone through the village for Mrs Simpson knew nothing about her.

'The first thing you do,' stated Jinny's mother, 'is to get out of those soaking clothes, dry yourself thoroughly and have something hot to eat.'

'I can't waste all that time! I've got to start and look for her now.'

'You're absolutely sodden. Have some sense. Getting pneumonia isn't going to help Shantih.'

'But anything could be happening to her,' said Jinny, staring desperately up at her mother.'

'Jinny,' warned her father. 'Get on with it and we'll all help you to look when you're ready.'

Defeated, Jinny kicked off her wellingtons, peeled off her oilskins and ran out of the kitchen. Passing the phone she thought of Clare. Shantih knew that there was a strange horse at Craigvaar. She might have gone there looking for Gatsby. Jinny grabbed the directory, found Clare's number, dialled it and waited, listening to the bell ringing out; tense to hear Clare's voice answering, telling her that Shantih was safe in one of her looseboxes. But there was no reply.

Jinny, gulping down a mug of scorching hot broth, eating a cheese sandwich, listened to her father.

'Mike's going to ride Bramble down to the shore and round to the farm. Search there.'

'I've just fed him,' said Jinny dismally.

'Correction,' said Mike. 'I'm going to walk.'

'We'll go up to the moors,' said her father, meaning Jinny and himself. 'And Mum will stay here in case anyone phones. It's almost half six now. We all come back here for nine.'

Mike nodded. Jinny said nothing. If they hadn't found Shantih she wasn't coming back.

Mr Manders, Mike and Jinny put on dry, waterproof clothing and stuffed their pockets with slices of bread.

'It will be all right,' said her mother, hugging Jinny. 'Shantih won't have gone far. She has too much sense.'

But Jinny shook her head, a lump stuck in her throat. For that kind of common sense was something that Shantih did not have. Bramble had it but not Shantih.

'She was out on the moors for bloomin' months when

she came here at first,' Mike grumbled as they went down to the stables to collect halters. 'Bet you if you left her she'd come back by herself.' He felt that his whole Saturday had been ruined by Jinny and her nonsense.

Jinny ignored him. She handed out halters, then tugged at her father's arm, hurrying him back to the house and then on to the moors. As they followed the track, Ken came running to catch them up.

'Just back,' he said. 'Your mum told me.' He had been visiting a pottery exhibition with Nell. 'She'll not have gone far in this weather.'

But Jinny knew that in wild weather Shantih loved to race against the wind, challenging the storm gods. On a mild day she might have wandered about Finmory but on a day like this she would have made for the highest reaches of the moor.

'Better split up,' suggested Ken when the track lost itself in the rough moorland.

Jinny saw her father give Ken a hard look.

'I'll go this way,' he said. 'You stick with Jinny and go towards Loch Varrich,' and Jinny knew that she wasn't to be left alone to search.

'Horse or no horse, we are all back at Finmory for nine. Understood?'

'He knows I won't come back if we haven't found her, that I couldn't leave her on the moors all night,' thought Jinny rebelliously.

'Right?' insisted Mr Manders, forcing Jinny to mutter, 'Of course.'

Ken and Jinny moved across the moor separated but keeping each other in sight. Over and over again Jinny called Shantih's name into the grey veils of rain. Her ears stretched for any sound that might be the clatter of hooves; her eyes straining for a glimpse of Shantih's red-gold shape.

Once Jinny was certain that it was Shantih sheltering by a pile of boulders. Stumbling through the dead heather Jinny dashed towards her; her whole being filled with delight – she could almost feel the strong bulk of Shantih, see her wide eyes glistening and hear her whicker of welcome.

'Shantih!' Jinny screamed.

A current of wind changed direction and the shape of the Arab fanned out into blown bracken fronds.

The rain grew less, changing into a steady drizzle. The grey mist still breathed across the moors changing the familiar ground into an insubstantial dream landscape. Wretchedly Jinny searched on, telling herself that in the next moment Shantih would hear her voice and come galloping to her.

Ken waved both arms above his head, signalling, and for a second hope leapt in Jinny. He had found Shantih. But when she waved back to let him know that she had seen him, he came leaping down the hillside to her.

'Half eight,' he said. 'Need to go back.'

'But we haven't found her,' Jinny said, turning away from Ken, her voice trembling into tears. 'We can't go back and leave her out here.'

'They may have found her. She may be back in her box, while we're wandering about up here. And you promised Tom.'

Reluctantly Jinny allowed herself to be persuaded. There was a chance that Ken was right. They might have found Shantih. But in her heart of hearts Jinny felt sure that her horse would not be on the shore or beyond the farm. Shantih would have made for the high places. In her mind's eye Jinny saw her galloping wildly up the hillside, her red-gold darkened to sorrel-rust by the rain, her eyes staring from her head, in frantic, driven speed.

'Not a hoofprint on the sand,' Mike said. 'No sign of her round the farm. She hadn't been there at all.'

Nor had Mr Manders found any sign of her.

Jinny stood beside the Aga, hands behind her back, her nails biting into her arm. Whatever happened she mustn't panic. Must not let them see what she was really feeling.

'It's a mild night and the rain's stopped,' said her father. 'Shouldn't think she'll come to any harm.'

Jinny nodded her head as if she was agreeing with him. She must not arouse their suspicions in case they made her promise not to go out again to search for Shantih. For of course she could not leave Shantih out on the moors all night. When her family were asleep Jinny was going out again.

'You're very quiet,' said Petra suspiciously, as they all sat round the table eating Mrs Manders' mushroom quiche. 'Normally if that horse sneezes you're nagging on at Dad to get the vet. Not like you a bit.'

Petra had only come home that evening. She had stayed on at school for extra music classes.

'If you had spent all day marching through Inverburgh instead of sitting on a piano stool, and three hours on the moors, you wouldn't be quiet, you'd be unconscious.'

'I would never be so childish as to go round asking people to sign a rubbishy petition to stop a motorway that has been absolutely certain for months.'

'Must have been last September when I first noticed a bit about it in the papers,' said Mrs Manders and their chat left Shantih alone, flowing on to talk about the state of the local roads and the garage's opinion of Mr Manders' car.

When she had done the dishes with Mike, Jinny told everyone that she was going to bed and went up to her room. She stood in front of the Red Horse.

'Where is Shantih?' she asked. Although the rain had

stopped the wind still blustered and whined around the house. Through the window Jinny could see the half moon buffeted by riding clouds. 'Please,' she pleaded, 'where is she?'

But the Horse was no more than a picture painted on the wall. Jinny walked through to the other half of her room and sat down on the edge of her bed.

'Need to wait until they're all asleep,' she thought. 'May as well read for a bit.'

Finding *The Sword in the Stone*, which was funny and interesting and different, Jinny propped up her pillows, took off her shoes and settled down under her duvet to read.

At first in her dream there was nothing but bright, scum-green which became one of the moor's most treacherous bogs. Then there was a rowan tree growing from a sheer rock fall behind it and the casual scatter of enormous boulders, some the size of a garden shed, that were strewn about the grass beside the bog. Jinny knew exactly where it was. She seemed to be watching it from a great height and yet she could see the least detail perfectly – the tracery of a moth's wing, the precise pattern in the saffron-coloured lichens encrusting the boulders or the brilliant ruby eye of a grouse pressed down into the heather. Then Shantih came walking out across the bald sheep-nibbled ground.

Jinny called her name in delight but Shantih gave no sign that she could hear her. She picked fastidiously at the withered grass and the dead reeds that sprouted from the firmer ground.

'Shantih,' Jinny screamed. 'Shantih.'

The sound of her own voice woke Jinny. She lay shuddering, arms wrapped round herself in terror, for in the split second before she woke Jinny had seen the dark figure of the Walker moving at Shantih's side.

Springing up, Jinny tore downstairs. The stone grey light of very early morning filled the house. She pulled on her wellingtons and anorak, and snatching up one of the halters that had been left at the back door she ran towards the moor.

Vaguely she realized that she must have fallen asleep but as she forced herself to keep on running against the rise of the moors Jinny was fully aware of only one thing – that Shantih was in danger, that her dream had warned her that she must reach her at once or it would be too late.

Jinny swung to her left, skirting the base of Finmory Beag and raced up the brow of a hillside to where a ridged backbone of crumbling stone wall stretched across the moor. From the wall the land rolled far down to a peaty burn then rose again in a wide sweep to the skyline. Stumbling, falling, gasping for breath, Jinny reached the burn, squelched through it and on up the heathered slope. From the top of the hillside the moor was textured with boulders, sudden rock falls scattered over the soft soil of the peat tussocks.

Even in her desperation Jinny was afraid to risk going straight across. She picked her way round the rocky edges of the bogs, scrabbled and pulled herself over the rocks and scrambled over slopes of ribbed rock to where the ground fell away again to moorland littered with the huge boulders that Jinny had seen in her dream.

Somewhere behind the clouds the sun had risen for the grey air was luminous now and the brilliant, deadly surface of the bog glowed eerily in its light.

But, grazing close to the edge of the bog, Shantih was safe.

Jinny tore down towards her. She flung her arms wide, her mouth opened to call Shantih's name, as her foot caught against a stone and the ground leapt up at her.

For moments she lay winded, unable to move or shout; only to lie staring at Shantih. Her reaching head, pricked ears and wide eyes were fixed on a flurry of new grass growing on a reedy hummock in the middle of the bog.

As totally helpless as if she had still been in her dream, Jinny saw Shantih stretch out her neck trying to reach the grass, hesitate, then step into the deadly fluorescence of the bog.

There was nothing beneath the surface for Shantih to stand on. Instantly her leg sank to above her elbow, tipping her whole body sideways as she struck out with her other foreleg, lifting it higher than a trotting pony's. When her hoof struck the scum of the bog it splattered the surface into jewelled splashes of light and then sank inexorably down.

Jinny half crawled, half staggered towards Shantih, shouting wildly to her. Hearing her voice Shantih whinnied through fear-blown nostrils, her eyes enormous with terror. She fought with straining quarters to free her forehand but her hind legs slipped and sank into the soft ground at the bog's edge.

In the minute it took Jinny to reach Shantih her chest had sunk into the bog and at her withers her mane was fanned out over the green slime.

Jinny's mind was on automatic pilot. She acted without thought. She knew that she had to get a halter on Shantih. Mr MacKenzie's warnings, her father's instructions came to the front of her mind and yet there were no words. She dragged fallen branches from a rowan tree, piled them at the edge of the bog, then flung herself flat on top of them; edged forward and fumbled the rough rope halter over Shantih's head. Beneath the branches Jinny could feel the trembling pull of the bog as she fought to knot the halter rope then squirm back to solid ground.

With raging violence she yelled at her horse, yanking

and pulling her whole weight on Shantih's head. At first Shantih plunged and struggled wildly, then, realizing that Jinny was trying to help her, she waited while Jinny paused and fought her hardest when Jinny pulled the rope. Once it seemed she had found some footing in the depth of the bog, for she rose up, chest and shoulders lifting free of the green slime, her weight carried on her quarters. But her hind legs were stuck too deeply into the soft ground at the edge of the bog and with a knife edge scream she sank back, the raddled, green slime closing over her withers.

Jinny stood shivering violently. She did not know what to do next; did not know what else she could do. To try to fetch help was useless for Shantih would have sunk out of sight by the time she got back. Yet to do nothing would mean that she would have to stand watching helplessly, while her most loved horse was sucked down in front of her eyes.

'Please God,' Jinny prayed. 'Please God save her.' Jinny shouted her agonized terror into the bleakness of the moors. 'Save her,' she demanded. 'Save her.'

A kind of madness seized Jinny, for she knew that she could not stand watching Shantih sink into this mire. If Shantih could not break free Jinny would plunge into the bog herself in a desperate attempt to keep Shantih's head above the slime. Although she knew it was impossible, that she would drown herself, she would not be able to stand and watch and do nothing.

And then she heard the sound – the whinnying speech that froze the blood in her veins. It was the Walker's voice. He was somewhere behind her calling Shantih's name with a high, night-bird calling.

Shantih heard him at once and answered, screaming her terror.

Again the Walker called.

Shantih gathered her strength and flung her head, snorting furiously. She plunged with all her strength, the muscles of her quarters knotted and strained. Sinking into the edge of the bog she seemed to find a standing place. Again she snorted, shuddered, rose up to the Walker's calling and with a final effort she exploded from the mire. Her hind legs held as she lashed round and plunged onto the ground.

Jinny forced her away from the bog and collapsed on the ground; lay shaking uncontrollably, unable to say anything except Shantih's name over and over again.

When at last Jinny was able to stand up and look round there were only sheep and the occasional hoodie crow to be seen. No black shape waited for Jinny beside the boulders or by the cliff and yet it was the Walker's cry that had saved Shantih; had given her the strength to free herself from certain death.

Jinny, plastered with peaty mud, threw her arms round Shantih's neck, ignoring the dripping slime in which she was covered. She had to feel her horse real and safe and alive.

A crow flew up from one of the boulders making Jinny's heart somersault into her throat. She doubled up Shantih's rope and in a sudden panic forced her away from the bog.

Once she had made sure that Shantih wasn't hurt Jinny hurried her on towards Finmory. Her head was filled with terror-bright flashes of the chestnut Arab sinking under the green slime of the bog. But it hadn't happened. It was over and Shantih was safe.

Above Finmory a slim, dark girl was walking across the moor, throwing sticks for a small, white, yapping dog. The girl saw Jinny, waved and came towards her. It was Kim, Clare's groom.

'The pits,' thought Jinny, for the last thing she wanted

69

was Clare Burnley hearing that Shantih had been trapped in a bog. But unless she turned round away from Finmory she could not avoid Kim.

The Jack Russell terrier came shooting over the bracken to bark around Shantih.

'Sprog,' shouted Kim. 'Come back here,' and the dog bounced back to her.

'Morning,' she called to Jinny. 'What a mess! Guess you've changed your mind then?'

'Changed my mind?' Jinny echoed.

'About turning her out on the moor,' replied Kim. 'That's what Clare said. Thought it a bit odd myself when you've entered for the ride. Your horse came galloping over to Craigvaar yesterday morning, screeching her head off to Gatsby. I was going to put her in one of our boxes but Clare chased her off. Said you always let her run wild for a week or two at this time of year.'

Jinny stared at Kim in open-mouthed disbelief.

'Never!' she exclaimed. 'I never let Shantih run loose on the moors.'

'When Clare chucked the gravel at her she went breezing off up the hills. "Quite used to being loose", that's what Clare said,' and with a lift of an eyebrow, a shrug of her shoulder, Kim let Jinny know what she thought of Clare.

CHAPTER SEVEN

When Jinny reached home she wisped Shantih down, managing to wipe off most of the drying slime. She checked her over carefully, making sure that she hadn't hurt herself, fed her and turned her out with Bramble. Jinny stood watching Shantih roll, shake herself and roll again before she began grazing.

'You're fine,' Jinny said, filled with relief to see Shantih safely back in her field.

'And now,' she thought darkly as she ran up to the house. 'Now for Clare Burnley.'

Jinny shed her outdoor clothes in the front porch, intending to go upstairs, change and ride Bramble over to Craigvaar at once but Petra's shout alerted her family to Jinny's return.

'Jinny!' Petra cried, coming downstairs to be confronted by Jinny's muddied appearance. 'What's happened to you? You're absolutely covered in filth. Are you all right? You look awful!'

Mrs Manders and Mike came hurrying out of the kitchen to stare at Jinny.

'Wherever have you been?' demanded her mother.

'Found Shantih,' said Jinny, wondering if she could make a bolt for it past Petra.

'We thought that's where you'd be,' said Mike.

'Do not breathe,' ordered her mother and she went to find a plastic bag for Jinny's clothes.

'Hot bath,' she said when they had all listened to Jinny's story. 'Then bed and I'll bring you up something to eat.'

'I'm not going to bed,' Jinny said. 'I'm not ill. And I told you I wasn't out all night or anything like that.'

'Bath first,' said her mother. 'And your hair.'

Grudgingly Jinny did what she was told.

'Wasting time when I should be telling Clare what I think of her,' she raged to herself as she rinsed her hair. 'I'm not going to bed. I'm going to Craigvaar.'

But by the time she had dried her hair it suddenly seemed quite a good idea to have breakfast in bed.

'You look a bit better now,' Petra said when she had brought a tray of tea and toast up to Jinny. 'Under the mud you were as white as a sheet.'

'If Shantih hadn't managed to get out herself there was nothing I could have done to save her,' said Jinny, shuddering at the memory.

'I expect there was,' said Petra, perching on the edge of Jinny's bed, 'only you didn't know what to do. I'm reading a library book at school which tells you exactly what to do in emergencies. Every night I learn what to do in three different emergencies. So I'll always be prepared.'

Jinny gulped at her hot tea, scalding her mouth to stop herself laughing out loud at Petra. She had a sudden picture in her mind of Petra sitting crisply upright in her school hostel bed, her hair newly shampooed, her face covered in cold cream, her nightdress frilly about her shoulders while she learnt how to get out of a submerging car or what to do when a bull was charging at you across a treeless plain.

'I'll lend it to you if you like,' Petra offered and Jinny realized that she must have been looking pretty shaken if Petra was being so pleasant.

'It was all Clare Burnley's fault,' said Jinny. 'Chasing Shantih back on to the moors.'

Normally Petra would have pointed out that it was Jinny's fault for not bolting the gate but she didn't.

'It sounds to me,' she said, 'as if Clare is scared you'll beat her. Wants to put Shantih out of action.'

And because it was Petra who said it, Petra who never, ever, took any interest in Jinny's horsey activities, Jinny thought about what she'd said and wondered if she might be right.

It was the afternoon before Jinny, riding Bramble bareback, trotted up the track to Craigvaar. After Petra had gone Jinny had snuggled back under the bedclothes and had not woken until her mother had called her down for lunch. As she passed Craigvaar's front door Jinny stared straight ahead. She didn't want to be stopped by Mr or Mrs Burnley. She did not want to waste her rage on anyone except Clare.

As she approached the stable yard at the foot of the long garden, Jinny heard Clare shouting at Gatsby.

'She's here,' Jinny thought with satisfaction and kicked Bramble on.

Clare, hearing hooves, came to the box door. Jinny halted Bramble and sat staring at her, hate and temper rising in her.

'You chased Shantih back on to the moor,' Jinny accused. 'She was nearly killed; nearly sucked down into a bog. And it was your fault.'

'Gracious,' said Clare. 'What is upsetting us now? We are in a knicker twist.'

Clare was wearing orange cords and a red sweater decorated with rows of regimented sheep. Her bland face under its froth of blonde curls smiled falsely up at Jinny.

'When you saw Shantih at your fence yesterday, you chased her off. Kim told me. It was a rotten, despicable thing to do. No one else would have done a thing like that.'

73

'So that's what all the fuss is about. I didn't want her disturbing Gatsby. She is so utterly bonkers she would upset any normal horse. Tearing up and down the fence neighing her head off.'

'You told Kim that I always turn her out on the moor. You know that's not true.'

Clare's loud, high-pitched laughter blotted out Jinny's words.

'But surely that is what you do? Surely I remember you telling me how she ran wild over the moors. I was only doing what I thought best.'

'That's it,' stormed Jinny. 'You were doing what you thought best, all right. Bloomin' best for you. You wanted her to be hurt. You wanted her to injure herself so that she wouldn't be fit for the ride. That's what you wanted because that's what would have suited you.'

'Do not be so utterly ridiculous,' sneered Clare. 'As if that weed of an Arab would be any competition for Gatsby.'

'Arabs are the best horses for long distance,' shouted Jinny. 'And you know it. All the books say so.'

'There are,' said Clare, speaking slowly, aiming her words at Jinny, 'Arabs and Arabs.'

'And Shantih is the best of them all,' Jinny shouted, twisting her fingers through lumps of Bramble's haystack mane to stop herself jumping down and thumping Clare.

'How touching,' mocked Clare. 'You really do believe that. Well, we will find out after the ride, won't we? That will give you the chance to show us all how brilliant your precious Arab is.'

'Right,' said Jinny. 'It will,' and she hauled Bramble round and kicked him into a battering trot.

Jinny pushed him on along the Craigvaar track and out on to the road to Finmory.

'She knew what she was doing when she chased Shantih

74

back on to the moors,' Jinny raged to Bramble. 'Petra was right. She did it to stop Shantih entering the ride. She didn't care what happened to her,' and Jinny saw again Shantih's fear-drawn face as she struggled to free herself from the bog.

When she turned Bramble out Jinny groomed Shantih in the field, choking on the clouds of dust that rose about them. As she groomed Jinny checked again to make sure that Shantih had not hurt herself.

'That Clare Burnley is the most foul, loathsome cow,' Jinny muttered to Shantih. 'But we'll show her that you are a million times better than her carthorse. Just let her wait.'

Thinking vaguely about homework Jinny went up to her room. She sat on her windowsill staring down at Shantih and Bramble grazing peacefully.

'Could have been dead,' she thought. The green slime smooth again and Shantih dead beneath it.

Jinny's hatred of Clare blazed within her. She was too agitated to settle to homework. Swinging about her room, shaking her hair, she decided to paint.

Jinny set out her paints, brushes and paper on her table, fetched water and sat down to stare at the blank paper waiting for a picture to form itself in her mind – Shantih plunging free from the bog; Shantih galloping through the moorland night; Clare – experienced, arrogant – laughing down at Jinny from the height of Gatsby. These images came and went through Jinny's head but would not stay. The image that came and refused to go away was of stone walls crashing to the ground; the seemingly indestructible walls of the Wilton crumbling to ruin.

In greys and blacks, the mute colours of destruction, Jinny painted the explosion of the stone walls. As she painted her rage gave way to a bleak despondency, to a barren hopelessness. Jo Wilton was dying. Would soon be dead. She could not save the Wilton. Most certainly it would be demolished. The Golden Horses would fall to dust. No one would ever see them dance again.

When she had finished Jinny stood back to look at the picture she had painted. Stone walls crashing to ruin in a black landscape of desolation.

As she looked at the picture Jinny froze with fear, bit on her clenched fist to stop herself screaming. To one side of the ruined building a figure in black clothing was standing; watching, waiting. Without being conscious of it Jinny had painted the Walker into her picture.

Staring mesmerized at her painting Jinny acknowledged the fact that she had not mentioned to her family; had hardly admitted to herself: the Walker had been on the moor that morning. It had been the Walker's voice that had given Shantih the power to save herself.

CHAPTER EIGHT

'Jinny!' called Dolina, her voice sharp with irritation. 'Would you hear what I'm shouting?'

Jinny jerked awake from a dream of Shantih winning one of the top long distance rides which she had read about in a book which had been waiting for her in Inverburgh Library.

'What?' she asked vaguely, looking round for Dolina amongst the crush of children waiting to go in to school dinners.

'It is that fancy woman,' said Dolina, pushing her way through to Jinny. 'Standing at the school gates, asking if anyone knows you.'

'Nell!' exclaimed Jinny, and without waiting to hear any more from Dolina she ran to the school gates.

'Jo Wilton?' she demanded, as she reached Nell.

'No, it's all right,' said Nell. 'He hasn't died. He wants to see you.'

'Me. Especially me?' Jinny asked, feeling a twist of fear in the pit of her stomach and hating herself for feeling like that about Jo Wilton.

'I was over this morning saying goodbye and he was asking to see you. I promised him I'd let you know. I've got to get back. Ben is beginning to feel somewhat neglected.'

'You're going away already? But we've hardly seen you.'

'Been jetting around,' said Nell. 'Perhaps we'll both come over in the summer. Have a real holiday.'

But to Jinny her words sounded empty. Nell had

changed. She might come or she might not. Whatever happened it wouldn't be the old Nell. She had gone forever.

Nell hugged Jinny, kissing her goodbye.

'You'd better go and see Jo as soon as you can. He has something to tell you,' she said. 'And don't break your heart over the Wilton. It has to come down. You can't stop it.'

Jinny stood waving, watching Nell's afro, dyed blonde hair and patchwork cloak grow small in the distance.

'Once she would have been with me,' Jinny thought. 'Doing everything she could to stop them touching the Wilton. She could have stopped them. But she doesn't care now. Not really.'

The bell rang for school dinners and automatically Jinny turned to answer it. Then she stopped, thought that the afternoon was only two supervised lessons in the Hall. She would go and see Jo Wilton now.

Jinny rang the door bell of Andrew Wilton's house and waited. Being ignored by Andrew Wilton when she had been there with Nell and Ken didn't make her feel that he would be overjoyed to see her again. But to Jinny's relief it was the lady who had brought in the coffee that answered the door.

'You've come to see old Mr Wilton,' she said, welcoming Jinny into the hall. 'Wait here a minute until I let nurse know.'

Jinny stood, twisting a strand of hair between her fingers, wondering what Jo Wilton wanted to say to her. She tried not to worry about how ill he was, what he would look like – only to remember that she loved him, that he was part of the mystery of the Red Horse.

'In you come,' beckoned the coffee lady and Jinny followed her along a corridor decorated with photographs of plastic people posing in front of cameras.

78

—

'Oh good,' said the nurse, smiling at Jinny. 'He's been fretting to see you. Something important he wants to tell you,' and she led Jinny across the bedroom to the double bed where Jo Wilton was lying propped up by pillows.

'Jo,' said the nurse. 'Here she is. Here's Jinny.'

The old man opened his eyes very slowly. He gazed distantly about the room, being called back from a far place to these unfamiliar surroundings. Then he recognized Jinny. His eyes lit up and it was the Jo Wilton Jinny knew who was looking at her. His bony hand closed on Jinny's arm, its feather touch trying to pull her down closer to him.

Jinny saw his lips move but she could not hear what he was saying. She bent over, listening intently.

'The best,' he said quite clearly, smiled and was asleep again.

'I couldn't hear him properly.'

'Don't worry,' said the nurse. 'He was really pleased to see you. He'll get some rest now.'

Jinny let herself out and caught an Inverburgh bus almost at once. She sat numbly, seeing nothing. She had intended to stay on until the bus station and get a bus straight home but almost without realizing what she was doing Jinny got off the bus at Carna Street and walked slowly, left foot, right foot, through the hazy spring afternoon towards the Wilton.

'What did he mean?' she asked herself. 'What was best about any of the things that were going to happen? Best that Jo Wilton was old and dying? Best that these gracious and seemly buildings were to be pulled down to make way for the poisonous roar of motorway madness? Best that the sanctuary of the Wilton would be no more, its treasures scattered, the magic of her painting turned to dust and debris? What could be best about any of this?'

On a rough piece of ground just past the Wilton a JCB stood alone. No human slaves attended it. Only the vast, metal destroyer; its jaws closed over serrated rows of metal teeth; its metal neck supine as it brooded silently waiting for the time when it would be energized for destruction.

On the door of the Wilton was a notice stating that due to a demolition order the Wilton Collection had closed and its contents had been distributed to other museums.

Jinny stared at it in disbelief. Although people had been telling her that the demolition was due to start any day she had not taken in the obvious fact that the Wilton would be closing down. Black curtains were drawn across the windows. There was no way that Jinny could see inside.

'The Horse god and Epona,' she said aloud. 'They can't have gone!' and she banged on the solidity of the door with her clenched fists, making a futile tapping sound.

'But I must see them again. I *must*. I must see the Golden Horses!'

Jinny ran down the row of tenements until she came to the end of the block and she was able to go round to the back of the buildings. The back yards were a neglected waste ground. Battered dustbins lay on their sides, the ground strewn with their rotting or dried contents; a rusty, abandoned bike was propped against an erupting armchair; a washing machine and a television set lay uselessly, side by side. Obviously the tenements in Carna Street had been gradually emptying for some time. With a shock Jinny looked at them and realized that although the windows were still curtained nobody lived there any longer. Already the houses were dead.

Jinny was able to pick out the back of the Wilton by the black curtains that were drawn across all its windows. She looked helplessly up at them. The windows that were

80

ground level from Carna Street were now high above her head. At the rear of the tenements the basements were at ground level, and each basement window was guarded by its own metal railing.

Grasping the railing in front of one of the Wilton's windows Jinny pulled at it desperately and felt it move as the metal loosened from the crumbling concrete. Again and again she tugged frantically at it with every ounce of her strength until the railing came away from the concrete with a violence that threw Jinny to the ground.

She jumped to her feet and, crouching down, examined the window. It wasn't locked. If she smashed one of the panes of glass she would be able to reach through and open it. Scrabbling through the rubbish Jinny found a discarded spade. She stood as far to the side as she could then swung the spade against the window shattering the glass. She knocked away all the splinters of glass and carefully reached her hand in to lift the handle, then using the spade as a lever she forced the window open.

In minutes she was through the window and standing in the basement of the Wilton. Except for packing cases piled against the walls it was empty. Remembering a story she had read in which a man in an empty basement was attacked by a pack of rats, Jinny dashed for the door. It creaked open and opposite her were stairs, another door and then she was out in the corridor she knew well. But it was totally changed. The display cases stood with their glass tops propped against the wall. The only sign of their vanished contents were the darker patches on the sun-faded green baize. The walls, too, showed bright rectangular patches where pictures and maps had once hung. Jinny looked round in utter dismay. Everything had gone. The Wilton was completely empty.

Her running footsteps rang loud in the dusty silence as

Jinny raced down the corridor to the room where Epona and the Horse god stood together.

The room was completely bare. Even the display case had gone.

A sobbing gulp of misery choked in Jinny's throat. How had it all happened so quickly? Why hadn't she realized? Why hadn't she gone into the Wilton last Saturday to see the statues? It had still been open then. Why had nobody told her?

Jinny stared up at her painting, drinking in the simple horse shapes she knew so well. Shapes that under the first beams of the sun had risen from the cave's walls and thousands of years ago had been outlined in black and filled in with burning, fire colours and now they were to be destroyed for ever. The knowledge of this was an agony of desolation as intense as the certain knowledge that someday Shantih would be dead. It was an endless falling where there were no words to hold you up.

A draught stirred the heavy curtains, a crack of sunlight glinted into the room and infused the Golden Horses with breath. They lifted from the wall, were radiant beings of air and fire. At first rearing and bucking in their new element then rising in a spiralling dance of joy. And Jinny was no longer a watcher, she was no longer separate, no longer knew herself as part of the whole but was the whole itself, was nothing but joy.

At the extreme edge of Jinny's awareness there was the sound of a car stopping outside the Wilton; a car door slamming. The sound clawed Jinny back to the everyday world. The energy of the Horses was withdrawn, they were no more than a flat painting. In the same way Jinny felt herself confined again within her body; unable to see unless she looked through her eyes; only able to hear with her ears. But the knowing of the dance was more real than any outward happening.

Jinny turned and the Walker was standing by her side. In the same moment Jinny heard the door of the Wilton being unlocked and pushed open. For a moment Jinny stood transfixed. She was held by the gaunt cheeks and blank eyes of the Walker. She remembered with computer recall – not line by line or minute by minute but in a unit of total recall – how the Walker had told her that he served the Golden Horses; how he had led her to the cave and waited with her when she had first seen the dance; how, when she had painted the Horses on the wall of the Wilton, his voice had told her to give them eyes, to let them see; and remembering these things her fear of the Walker became a stupid, childish thing. She saw his dry lips move. Almost she stayed to listen.

The sound of footsteps coming along the corridor grew louder and Jinny lost herself in panic. She swung away from the dark figure and ran full tilt out of the room, not caring who it was that was approaching. Only wanting to be with another human being. Not to have to listen to the Walker's words.

'What on earth are you doing here?' Andrew Wilton demanded as Jinny hurtled towards him. 'How the hell did you get in? What's wrong with you?'

'There . . .' Jinny stood speechless in front of him. The last gleam of the dance was a vivid daze behind her eyes and her heart still thumped from the sudden terror of the Walker's appearance.

'Came to see my painting,' Jinny managed at last.

'The dickens you did!' exclaimed Andrew Wilton. 'And how did you get in?' he demanded again.

'Breaking and entering,' Andrew Wilton said when Jinny had finished her garbled explanation. 'But under the circumstances there's not much damage you could have done. I'm here to let the men in for the last of the display cases and that will be that. I'll be glad to see the back of this place. Nothing but a weight on my whole life. It was always to be left to my son before he took himself off to Nepal and finished himself off with dope.'

Andrew Wilton stopped abruptly, as if suddenly realizing who he was speaking to.

'Right. Out with you,' he said. 'And stay out.'

It wasn't until she was tacking up Shantih that Jinny let herself think about what she had done. She had danced the dance of the Golden Horses, known its utter joy and minutes later she had run away from the Walker because she was too afraid to listen to him. She had run to a dead person like Andrew Wilton because she had been afraid. If she had stayed, could the Walker have told her something that would have saved the Golden Horses?

Jinny drove the thought from her mind. Tomorrow was Saturday and Jinny was to ride Shantih over a twenty-mile route which Miss Tuke had planned. When Jinny got back to Finmory Miss Tuke would be waiting with the vet to check Shantih's heart beat and pulse rate.

'Fourteen days and it's the ride. Fourteen days to prove to Clare that you are better than Gatsby,' Jinny told Shantih as she mounted and began to ride home, settling Shantih into a steady trot; feeling Shantih centre herself, paying attention to her rider not flinching at the sudden appearance of sheep or passing cars.

'Fourteen days,' thought Jinny again. And in those fourteen days what would have happened? Where would Jo Wilton be? And the Golden Horses?

CHAPTER NINE

Miss Tuke arrived at Finmory shortly after nine on Saturday morning, just as the Manders were having breakfast. Jinny had been up at seven, had groomed Shantih, fed her and left her with a handful of hay. Shantih had known something was going to happen. She flaunted round her box, thrusting her chest against the half door, stretching her neck to follow Jinny.

'It's not that I've forgotten. I'm not thinking of turning you out,' Jinny told her. 'Be prepared, this is the beginning.'

Miss Tuke accepted Mrs Manders' offer of coffee. She sat down next to Jinny, shifting Mike up a place, and spread her plan of Jinny's route out on the breakfast table.

'We'll aim to start at eleven,' Miss Tuke told Jinny. 'Give her a quarter of an hour's schooling first. I'll see whether you've been doing any work or not. Twenty-mile ride and you're aiming at a speed between six and seven miles per hour. So time yourself to be back here about two.'

Jinny checked her watch; wound it, shook it then borrowed Mike's, knowing that her own was capricious. She would need to borrow it for the real ride.

'Been following the feeding sheet I gave you?'

Jinny nodded, not looking up at her father but hearing him groan.

'Young entry,' declared Miss Tuke. 'Must cheer them on. You'll never notice a few pounds here or there.'

'Not I,' said Mr Manders. 'It's the bank manager who has hang-ups about that sort of thing.'

'No trouble from mine,' said Miss Tuke. 'Shoots into his office like a bolting rabbit every time he sees me. Scared stiff I'll corner him.'

'I believe you,' said Mr Manders.

Jinny studied the route. She was to ride from Finmory to Glenbost then on to Ardtallon which was in the opposite direction to Inverburgh. Past Ardtallon she was to take a path through a forest which Miss Tuke had marked as 'Good going – canter.' Out of the forest it was rough going unfamiliar to Jinny, but Miss Tuke, out trekking, had marked the way with yellow markers. Down from the moorland to a clutch of five or six cottages, where Miss Tuke would meet her. After a stop she would ride on to the moor again, still following Miss Tuke's markers, until she saw Loch Varrich on her right when she would be on familiar ground and could make her own way down to Finmory.

Jim Rae the vet arrived as she was about to saddle up.

'I'll take a look at her now,' he said. 'And I'll be here for two to check her pulse and respiration rate after you've ridden her.'

Standing outside the stable, holding Shantih while Jim Rae checked her over, Jinny felt the first uneasy twist of nerves. Although everyone who finished the ride would receive a rosette it was a competition, with other people judging Shantih while Jinny waited tensely for their verdict on fitness and time.

'Fine,' said Jim Rae. 'Both heart and pulse rate normal,' and Jinny beamed her relief. He checked Shantih over for lumps, bumps or strains but again he could find nothing wrong.

'Trot her up for me,' and Miss Tuke, playing the part of helper, trotted Shantih up and down the path.

'Dead even,' said Jim Rae. 'No problem. She's looking great. I'll check her again when you've ridden her.'

Jinny schooled to Miss Tuke's satisfaction and at eleven o'clock set off towards Glenbost. She was to meet Miss Tuke at half past twelve. Shantih settled to a steady trot and it wasn't until she had reached Glenbost and turned towards Ardtallon that Jinny brought her back to a walk.

Jinny had ridden to Glenbost hundreds of times and to Ardtallon dozens of times but somehow today was quite different. She felt as if Miss Tuke and the vet were watching every stride Shantih took – Miss Tuke for pace and rhythm and the vet for soundness.

'It's only riding Shantih,' Jinny told herself. 'Like any other time,' but it wasn't. In two weeks' time she would be riding against Clare.

The gate into the forest was bolted and Jinny had to dismount and use all her strength to force it open. Once remounted she let Shantih canter on along the track between the marshalled pines, their resinous, musty smell filling her nostrils.

Riding through the forest took longer than Jinny had expected. It was after twelve before she rode away from the trees. Miss Tuke should have written gallop.

Once on the moor Jinny saw the first of Miss Tuke's yellow markers stuck into the ground. She trotted towards it and before she reached it the next marker was in sight. They led her across the moor until she came down to the cottages with Miss Tuke's van parked beside them and somehow Jinny was almost as relieved to see it as if she had been riding across Australia instead of being quite close to home.

Sitting in the back of Miss Tuke's van Jinny drank tomato soup but wasn't hungry. She watched as Miss Tuke practised being back-up team – loosening Shantih's girth, easing her saddle, letting her drink at a burn, checking her over for cuts or scratches and holding her reins while she ate the small feed that Miss Tuke had brought for her.

In half an hour Jinny was riding on to the moors again. After an undecided morning the sun had come out and Shantih gazed about her, alert to the new countryside.

'Bet you're wondering what all this is about,' Jinny said. 'A lot of fussing.'

Shantih whickered a reply to Jinny's voice and Jinny let her trot on, finding her way easily from marker to marker.

Long before Jinny had been expecting it there was a gleam of silver water to her right and they had reached Loch Varrich. Soon Jinny was back on what she thought of as her own moor. When she rode down to the stables Miss Tuke, her father and the vet were standing joking together.

'Perfect,' announced Jim Rae when he had finished checking Shantih. 'She hasn't even broken sweat. Must be pretty fit,' and leaving Jinny to see to Shantih they went into the house for a cup of tea.

'It had been good,' Jinny thought, grinning to herself. Really it had only been an ordinary, longish ride but when she had been cantering through the forest or following Miss Tuke's markers over the unknown moor, it had been a challenge that Jinny and Shantih had to meet together.

The final of the Golden Horseshoe Ride which had been shown on the Riding Club's video was a two-day ride of a hundred miles. The Tevis Ride in America followed the Pony Express trails over the Sierra Nevada in California. 'But then,' Jinny thought, 'there wouldn't be Clare.'

Jinny stood watching Shantih eating her feed, waiting to turn her out and wondering if she should clean her tack. Ken came into the stable. Jinny glanced up and although she had hardly thought of the Wilton all day,

88

not thought about it as the thing that was first in her mind, she knew at once what Ken had come to tell her.

'Is it Jo Wilton?' she demanded.

'We'd a phone call just now. Nell had asked them to be sure to let us know. He died in his sleep last night.'

Jo Wilton's funeral was on Tuesday morning. Jinny went with Ken. There was a long service in an Inverburgh church and the burial was in an old graveyard, textured with mossy headstones and memorials. Jinny watched with the tears tracking down her face. Then a blackbird landed on an angel and singing its heart out drowned the minister's words with a paean of joy.

Walking back to school Jinny passed the end of Carna Street and saw that men in overalls and gaudy hard hats were starting up the JCB. It was about to begin.

Next day Jinny took a packed lunch to school and ate it in Carna Street. She stood watching the metal monster jab and thrust at a stone wall; draw back and attack it again and again until there was a tremulous sigh in the strength of the wall, plaster trickled, blocks of stone balanced on air, then fell into crashing chaos. Tiles from the roof fell like autumn leaves as the roof beam shattered. Through the blinding curtains of dust the JCB roared in again, its metal jaws with their serrated teeth gaping to grab and pull and tear. Their rending exposed pathetic glimpses of wallpaper; or a kitchen dresser, revealed for minutes and then torn away into nothing.

When Jinny came back at lunchtime the next day only another two tenements had been destroyed and the cavernous jaws of the JCB was gulping mouthfuls of rubble and swinging it round to dump it into waiting lorries.

Jinny sat on the Wilton steps so lost in misery that when a down-and-out moved in beside her she didn't mind; was not afraid as she usually was but gave him some of her sandwiches and refused a drink from his bottle of cheap wine as if it had been Mike offering her lemonade.

Although she came at lunchtime for the rest of the week and could easily have crept into the Wilton through the basement window Jinny did not try to see the Golden Horses again. Partly it was fear of the Walker; partly because the memory of the dance was still so vivid in her mind she was afraid that seeing the painted horses would dull its magic; but more than any of these things it was the hopeless misery of knowing she could do nothing to stop the demolition. The Wilton was to be pulled down. In a way it was already destroyed. They – from Nell to her mother to Andrew Wilton – had all been right.

Jinny went to Carna Street after school on Friday afternoon to find the JCB abandoned and not a workman in sight. They had stopped for the weekend. Children were playing in the ruins; firing stones, having tea parties.

By this time next week, if the demolition continued at the same rate, they would have reached the Wilton. Jinny stood staring up at the blank, curtained windows, lost in a desolate misery. The little statues of the Celtic gods had gone and soon the Golden Horses would be destroyed and there would be no way to save them this time. Jinny turned and left it.

'Did you know that there are 50 billion supergiants in the Milky Way galaxy?' Mike asked as they rode home together.

'Who counted them?' asked Jinny scornfully. 'What about the stars humans can't see? Who counts them?'

'God,' suggested Mike and it seemed a more sensible possibility than any human counting 50 billion anythings.

Shantih pranced beside Bramble, irritated at being held back. The vitamin and mineral supplement and the high protein horse cubes which Miss Tuke had brought for

Jinny to add to Shantih's feeds had given her coat a new glossiness. She was fitter and stronger than ever before.

'Shall we go back over the moors?' Jinny suggested.

Mike shook his head. 'You can if you like. I promised Mr MacKenzie I'd help him with the sheep.'

Jinny rode Shantih on to the moors. Tomorrow she was taking Shantih over the same route as last Saturday but riding two miles past Ardtallon and then back which would mean she had ridden over twenty-four miles.

But tonight Jinny felt like a gallop over the moors. Forgetting about pace and rhythm; only to gallop. To gallop away Jo Wilton's death; to wipe out everything except her horse. Shantih flirted her hooves and clinked her bit, as keen to be galloping as Jinny herself.

'Steady a minute,' Jinny said, holding Shantih to a trot. 'Wait till we get to the long gallop and then we'll race.'

The long gallop was a reach of moor which Jinny had discovered. First there was a good, clear track through the bracken, then a long stretch of clean turf, a small wall and a final, slightly uphill, stretch of moorland. It ended in a stone wall which could not be jumped because of the scatter of rocks on the other side.

Whenever Jinny rode towards the start of the gallop Shantih knew where they were going. She bounded forward – half rearing, half bucking, trembling with anticipation.

'She'll be like this on the ride,' Jinny thought. 'Mad. Uncontrollable. Doesn't matter now but it will then. Don't care. Don't care about it now.'

At the top of the rise just before the gallop, seeming to fill the entire moor with her presence, was Clare on Gatsby. Jinny pulled Shantih up in disgust. Perhaps if she waited Clare would ride on without noticing her but Shantih reared up, twirling round in frustration.

'Still out of control?' Clare shouted, riding towards Jinny. 'She really is the limit, isn't she?'

Struggling to stay on, grabbing mane and saddle, Jinny could think of nothing to say in reply.

'Came up here to give him a pipe opener but I can't find a decent piece of ground. Not a thing but rabbit holes. I suppose you gallop anywhere but when one is on a valuable horse like Gatsby, one has to take a bit of care.'

'Of course I don't gallop anywhere, don't be so stupid,' snapped Jinny, her temper flaring. 'There's loads of places you can gallop.'

'Super,' said Clare. 'Let's go,' making Jinny feel that she had fallen into a trap which Clare had set.

'If there was any point in it I'd suggest a race but . . .' and Clare raised her eyebrows and made a gusty, disparaging noise.

'As if Shantih couldn't beat that carthorse!'

'Let's see then,' said Clare, clicking shut the door of her second successful trap.

'Right,' said Jinny and she pointed out the gallop to Clare, emphasizing that they must stop at the second wall.

'We'll need to go single file through the bracken and then we can race,' said Jinny. 'I'll lead. I know the way.'

As they came to the track through the bracken Jinny eased her touch on Shantih's reins and Shantih changed into a canter. Jinny sat down holding in her speed between seat and hands. The beat of Gatsby's hooves pounded behind them.

When they were free from the bracken Jinny checked Shantih, held her for a second until she felt, rather than saw, Gatsby's head drawing level with Shantih's shoulder. Then she released her hold on the reins and crouching forward over Shantih's withers gave her her head.

The wind of their speed bannered back Jinny's hair,

wisped Shantih's mane and strained the flesh of her head into a tense mask that seemed all eyes and flared nostrils. Gatsby pounded at their side, collected and confident. Clare urged him on and he lengthened his stride until, almost without realizing what had happened, Jinny was galloping with Gatsby's quarters bulked in front of her. Jinny's instinct was to ride wildly, urging Shantih on, but she remembered Miss Tuke's lectures on pace and rhythm and balancing your horse, and kept Shantih at a steady gallop just behind Gatsby.

Having ridden the gallop so often Jinny knew exactly where the low, stone wall was. She timed her take-off perfectly, sent Shantih soaring in a long, low arc, flying past Gatsby as he cleared the wall with feet to spare.

Jinny set her will to race to the finish, not to let Gatsby pass her again. Keeping Shantih's rhythm she urged her on and felt her respond, increasing her speed without any loss of balance. Gatsby strained to overtake them – laborious, earnest, he pounded on; while Shantih was a blown feather, a swallow's flight. As they reached the wall the two horses were neck to neck.

Scarlet in the face Clare pulled Gatsby to a halt. Shantih, knowing they always stopped at the wall, came sweetly to hand and Jinny, carried away by the thrill of their speed, turned to Clare grinning widely.

'That was great,' she cried. 'A super gallop!' And in that moment she was almost ready to be friends with Clare; even ready to forgive her for chasing Shantih back on to the moor and to look forward to the ride as something to be shared.

'Gallop!' jeered Clare and her mask of sophistication had vanished. It was a spiteful ten year old that Jinny saw looking out of her eyes. 'One might say that in your case it was more than a gallop. It was a runaway. As usual you were totally out of control.'

CHAPTER TEN

The next Friday at five o'clock Jinny was sitting on Finmory's front doorstep waiting for the arrival of Miss Tuke. They were to spend the Friday night before the ride with Miss Tuke's friend Laura Sims who lived, according to Miss Tuke, in an egg-cosy cottage that was conveniently close to the Brandoch Country Club where the Riding Club was based. The ride was to start from there at eleven o'clock on Saturday morning.

Jinny's case was packed and in the stable Shantih and her tack waited in gleaming perfection. Kelly, Ken's grey dog, was sitting beside Jinny. She drew him to her and he laid his shaggy head on her knee, gazing up at her with wise yellow eyes.

At lunchtime Jinny had gone to Carna Street as usual. They had almost reached the Wilton. It seemed to Jinny that in another day, even while she was competing in the long distance ride, the Golden Horses would shatter into dust. Then a workman had blown a whistle and the lumbering JCB had deposited its last load of rubble and, obedient as a circus elephant, had returned to its waste ground, lowered its head and slept. The workmen had climbed into a truck and been driven away. Before Jinny had gone back to school Carna Street was deserted; abandoned for the weekend. On Monday she would dog off school and come straight to Carna Street to watch and wait, to be sure she was there.

Jinny smoothed Kelly's ears, running them between her fingers, scratching under his chin so that he smiled, lifting up his lips in sheer pleasure. Almost Jinny wished that there was no long distance ride; wished that Miss Tuke would never come to collect her so that she could go now to keep watch over the Wilton. But that was stupid. She had seen the workman stopping for the weekend. There would be no more demolition until Monday. And there was Clare Burnley to think about – Miss Tuke had better come.

As if produced by Jinny's thought Miss Tuke's box came roaring into the drive.

'Here's Miss Tuke,' Jinny yelled, so that her parents would come out to chat to Miss Tuke while Jinny went to bring Shantih from the stable; Shantih looking poshed up in her yellow bandages.

'Are we going to have a performance?' asked Miss Tuke when she had lowered the ramp. 'Brought the box instead of the trailer. Thought it might make things easier. Now lead her up to the ramp. Give her time to have a good look inside, then twist her round sharply and up you go.'

Shantih stretched out her neck, breathing in the smells of all the trekking ponies that had travelled in the box, her ears sharp and suspicious as she stared into its treacherous darkness.

Jinny waited patiently until she felt her horse relax, then turned her round and strode confidently into the box talking briskly to Shantih as she did so. Head bowed, hooves clomping on the hollow ramp, Shantih walked mildly at her side. Jinny tied her up and Miss Tuke fitted a partition.

'Is this an omen, I ask myself?' said Miss Tuke. 'Usually the block and tackle if I remember correctly?'

'Has been known,' admitted Jinny, as relieved as Miss Tuke that Shantih had boxed without her usual carry-on.

'And what is Miss Burnley doing? Driving over tomor-

95

row morning?' Miss Tuke asked when they were lumbering towards Glenbost.

'Staying the night at Brandoch Country Club. Stabling Gatsby there,' said Jinny. 'Mr MacKenzie told me so it's bound to be right.'

After Glenbost Miss Tuke turned towards Inverburgh. Jinny had thought that Brandoch would be in the opposite direction, but when her mind was on something else she was perfectly capable of standing outside Mrs Simpson's shop and wondering which way to turn for Finmory, so she said nothing.

'Going this way,' said Miss Tuke, when Jinny didn't mention that they were driving in the wrong direction, 'to collect some tack. They promised to get it back to me by Wednesday. Phoned them up Wednesday afternoon and they couldn't deliver until next week. Said I'd collect it myself, tonight. Told them there would be trekkers without reins if I didn't. Could not have cared less. And that is what the world's come to!'

The saddler who had been stitching Miss Tuke's tack was in one of Inverburgh's back streets. It was a dim, dusty shop with vanishing gold lettering across its window. While Miss Tuke was rousing them up Jinny watched Shantih through the little window at the back of the cabin. She was standing calmly, picking absentmindedly at her hay net.

'Bet she wonders where she's going,' Jinny thought. 'That's how it is for animals. Everything normal then pow! – the long distance ride; sold or the slaughter house; absolutely anything. No dreading things or looking forward to things. Just happenings.' And Jinny wondered if perhaps animals knew something more than humans did; something greater than the comings and goings and changes of humans; some secret that let them live placidly in the madness of the human world.

Miss Tuke dumped a pile of stitched reins, stirrup leathers and girths in beside Jinny and heaved herself up into the driver's seat.

'Can't go the way I thought we could,' she said. 'One-way street now. Need to go round by Carna Street and out that way.'

Jinny stiffened. She had forced everything to do with the Wilton out of her mind. This weekend was to be Shantih, the ride and nothing else. The very last thing she wanted to do was to drive past the Wilton.

After twisting and turning along several back streets Miss Tuke drove into Carna Street. The tenements at this end were still untouched. They stood drowsing in their accustomed elegance, unaware of the approaching destruction.

As they drove up Carna Street Shantih gave a clarion whinny.

'What's up with her?' said Miss Tuke, and Jinny shuddered goose-over-her-grave at the sound, for they were approaching the Wilton.

Again and again Shantih screeched in strident waves of noise. Her hooves crashed against the side of the box as she fought to free herself.

'What the dickens!' cried Miss Tuke, slamming on the brakes. 'She'll have the bloomin' box smashed in. Give over! Enough of your nonsense!'

'Don't stop,' Jinny cried. 'Drive on and she'll be OK!'

'Drive on and I'll be driving matchwood,' answered Miss Tuke, jumping out of the cabin, yelling at Shantih to stop her nonsense. 'Got to get in to her.'

They lowered the ramp and Jinny sprang into the box to where Shantih stood, head high and crazed, straining against her halter while she lashed out with metal-shod hooves against the side of the box.

'Whoa, steady, Shantih. Whoa the woman,' Jinny

mouthed as she ducked under the partition and tried to grasp the halter. But Shantih ignored her presence and screamed again and again through cavernous nostrils. She lowered the weight of her quarters against the partition and it splintered and broke. She reared up against the halter rope fighting with all her power to free herself. Her hind hooves skidded on the floor of the box.

'Watch it, she's coming down,' yelled Miss Tuke.

For an instant Shantih seemed to hang suspended from her halter and in that instant Jinny grabbed at the end of the rope and pulled the quick release knot undone. Shantih surged upright – legs splaying and hooves skidding – and crashed her way over the broken partition. The halter rope burnt through Jinny's hands and Shantih was free. She leapt over the ramp and into Carna Street swinging round to charge across the road to the Wilton. A car coming fast in the other direction sounded his horn as he reached the box.

There seemed no way he could miss Shantih. Jinny saw her horse lying bleeding in the road. Then he was past and it had not happened. Shantih, frightened by the car, dragging her halter rope, bolted up Carna Street and into the traffic. She whirled and reared, filled with panic, desperately trying to get back to the Wilton but headed this way and that by the traffic. Jinny ran into the road. Cars streamed past. Then a horsebox driven by Clare Burnley.

'Help me! Help me!' Jinny screamed. 'Stop! Stop!' but Clare drove on.

This time Jinny heard the sound that she had not heard before although she had been sure that Shantih had heard it – the high, whinnying call of the Walker. Narrowly missing a lorry, sending a moped slanting into the kerb, Shantih was through the traffic and storming up Carna

Street to the Wilton; to stand in front of it staring up at its curtained windows.

Jinny reached Shantih before Miss Tuke. She grabbed the rope shouting love and fury at Shantih but her horse paid no attention, her whole being concentrated on the Wilton. Against her will Jinny felt herself forced to look up too. The curtains of one of the windows moved and the Walker stood there, looking straight down into Jinny's eyes.

Panting for breath, cursing, Miss Tuke arrived at Jinny's side.

'Is she all right?' she demanded. 'God knows how she wasn't killed. And how there wasn't the most almighty accident . . .'

For a moment Miss Tuke distracted Jinny and when she looked up at the window again the curtains were still and Shantih was standing relaxed and herself again.

'It wasn't her fault,' Jinny pleaded. 'Honestly she couldn't help it.'

'Sometimes I think you should have her checked for a brain tumour,' Miss Tuke said grimly and Jinny longed to be able to explain but knew there was no way that Miss Tuke would ever understand.

Together they looked Shantih over but apart from a surface scratch on her off fore she was unharmed.

'Let's hope she isn't lame for the vet tomorrow,' said Miss Tuke. 'What am I doing encouraging you in this . . .?'

'Did you see Clare?' Jinny demanded, suddenly remembering. 'She drove past when Shantih was in the road. She *must* have seen her and she never stopped.'

'Thank you,' said Miss Tuke. 'I have remembered why I'm here.'

Jinny stayed in the back of the box with Shantih who

had boxed obediently and travelled quietly for the rest of the journey.

Laura Sims, Miss Tuke's friend, had a loosebox ready for Shantih. Although her cottage was egg-cosy neat it was architect-designed modern and built in what had once been the grounds of a large estate. Her garden contained two old-fashioned looseboxes which she used as a garage and garden shed. For Shantih she had cleared and converted her garden shed into a loosebox. Shantih approved. She settled without any fuss, hardly bothering to look up when they left her.

Miss Tuke hurried them through their baked beans on toast, then they all got into Laura's Mini and drove down to the Country Club. Miss Tuke, plan in hand, pointed out the start of the ride which was clearly marked with luminous orange tape. Then they drove on stopping at vantage points where Miss Tuke and Jinny got out and climbed over gates or crossed fields so that Jinny could see the way she was going to ride tomorrow. Roughly halfway through the ride there was a compulsory stopping place where Miss Tuke and Laura would be waiting, ready to spring into action as back-up support team.

Jinny said 'Yes' and 'No' at the right times; tried to listen to Miss Tuke's instructions on where she could canter, or where she should walk, or keep Shantih to a strong ground-eating trot, but it was all as if she was sitting in a cinema watching a film and somehow being made to take part in it at the same time. She didn't want to be here with Miss Tuke and Laura, no matter how kind or charming they were being. Jinny only wanted to be back with Shantih, to be alone with her horse, to have time to think about the Walker standing black against the dark curtains of the Wilton, trying to tell Jinny some secret thing.

Jinny thanked Laura when she showed her into her

chintzy bedroom and made polite appreciative remarks about Laura's home-made lentil pie and Baked Alaska.

'Could I go down and say goodnight to Shantih,' Jinny said, getting up from the supper table as soon as she could.

When they had come back from looking at the route Laura had parked her Mini and Miss Tuke had led Shantih out but she had showed no sign of stiffness or strains. While Jinny groomed, Miss Tuke had filled her water bucket and hay net, given Shantih a feed and hurried Jinny into the house where Laura was waiting.

Now, released from the supper table, Jinny ran over the smooth lawns, leaping flower beds of spring bulbs.

'Shantih,' she called. 'Shantih,' and Shantih's bright, brittle face welcomed her over the half door of Laura's garden shed.

Jinny let herself in and threw her arms round Shantih's neck.

'You knew he was there, didn't you?' she whispered. 'You'd have kicked your way out of that box to reach him.'

And Jinny saw again the dark figure of the Walker standing in the curtained window staring down at her. But there had been no terror in the Walker's gaze. His eyes had carried a look that Jinny had seen once before. Knew she had seen it but could not place it or understand it. She stood leaning against Shantih desperately trying to remember.

Laura and Miss Tuke came strolling through the garden laughing together.

'Up at dawn tomorrow,' Miss Tuke said when they reached Jinny. 'Thought we'd better come and dig you out,' and with her words Jinny remembered.

The look in the Walker's eyes had been the same as the

expression Jinny had seen in the eyes of the Celtic pony folk when, in her vision, she had seen them watching helplessly as the archaeologists' dig came closer to the place where their Horse god was buried; when they were asking for Jinny's help.

CHAPTER ELEVEN

Tight with nerves, Jinny sat astride Shantih as her horse spun round in rearing circles. Already several groups of horses had started out on the ride. Each time a group had left, Shantih had thought she was going with them and each time she had been left behind she had got more and more excited.

It had been a grey, misty morning and wreathing mist still breathed around the hills. Jinny, who had more or less convinced herself that it would be much the same as a pony trek only faster, had been stunned by the numbers taking part. They all seemed as confident and professional as Clare and they all seemed to know each other and to talk in loud voices about pulse rates and respiration.

Miss Tuke had been unshakable. 'Shantih is as good as any of them,' she had said but Jinny knew it was only part of her back-up team duties and not what she really thought about Shantih.

Miss Tuke had driven the box to the Club and parked it there. Once Jinny had started, Miss Tuke and Laura would drive to the halfway halt in Laura's Mini. In the back of the Mini was a box in which Miss Tuke had collected everything she might need as back-up crew, from scissors to hay. She was ready for any emergency.

Gatsby and Clare started with a group of five other riders. Although Clare was only wearing a crash cap and casual clothes like all the other riders Clare's were casually expensive. Gatsby's style and breeding gave him a presence that set him apart from the others.

'Dare say he cost her father a bomb,' said a knowledgable voice. 'But is he the horse for long distance?' and Jinny's heart warmed to the unknown man.

At a steady loping trot Gatsby led the way across the field, down the avenue of trees, vanishing into a bank of mist before he reached the end of the avenue. Two more starts and then it would be Jinny.

'Lost you,' said Miss Tuke, striding towards them and gripping Shantih's bit ring with a heavy hand. 'She's going to cart you the first mile or so but try to get her settled before the moorland. You don't want her running like a banshee over that. Break her neck or wear herself out before you reach halfway. Eh?' and Miss Tuke rattled Shantih's bit.

'How about yourself? Got over the jitters?'

Jinny nodded, feeling a fool. Normally she was never nervous on Shantih but this morning she had felt uptight and tense without really knowing what was wrong. It was not as if she had to jump or race or ride a cross-country course. She had just been scared of nothing.

But under the surface Jinny knew perfectly well what was wrong. She knew that once she had realized that the Walker needed her help she should have gone to Carna Street as soon as she possibly could.

'I'll go tomorrow morning,' Jinny had promised herself. 'Nothing can happen before that. The demolition has stopped for the weekend. Sunday morning will be soon enough.'

But as she sat waiting for the minutes to pass before she started, Jinny knew that it wasn't enough. She should have left behind all notion of proving to Clare that Shantih was a better horse than Gatsby. She should have made a fuss last night, found some way of making Miss Tuke drive her back to Finmory so that she could have been at the Wilton now.

'Take her up to the Start. They're ready for you.'

And with the sound of Miss Tuke's voice Jinny banished all thoughts of the Wilton from her mind, for really what difference could it possibly make whether she was there or not when the Golden Horses were destroyed?

'I'll count to three,' said the tweed-suited starter. 'Then you're off.'

'One,' she announced. 'Two,' and in the instant between her words the Walker's voice had echoed in Jinny's ears.

'You who were chosen to find the Horse god. You who know the power of the Red Horse. You who serve.'

'Three,' said the starter, and Shantih leapt forward fighting for her head. She plunged across the rough tussocky grass and reaching the mossy avenue between the trees stretched her neck out, leaning on the bit and galloping as if the hounds of hell were behind her.

At first Jinny tried sitting down in the saddle and sawing at Shantih's mouth in a useless attempt to bring her under control, but Shantih paid not the least attention.

Before they reached the patch of mist at the end of the avenue Jinny had left the others who had started at the same time as herself far behind and overtaken three riders from the start before her. She was helpless to control Shantih. But when they came out of the mist and Jinny saw the rolling moorland stretching enticingly before her she gave up, stopped trying to slow Shantih down and let her have her head to gallop on.

Shantih went like all things flying, following the orange markers at a full out gallop. After the rock and heather of Finmory's moors it was a delight to feel the short springing turf on the smooth undulating hills.

Gradually Shantih began to settle, although she was still galloping. Jinny was in control again.

From the hills the route led down a steep lane to a track by the side of a hurtling river, under a canopy of spring-green, silver birches and larches. The track was narrow, only wide enough to take one horse, so that everyone slowed down to a walk, a walk that stopped and started as riders who had reached the ford across the river refused to step down the banking into the water.

'My chap won't look at it,' moaned the woman riding a dun pony in front of Jinny. 'Lord knows when I'll get across.'

'Shantih won't mind. I'll give you a lead,' said Jinny, and when they came to the ford she urged Shantih past the dun pony and rode her down the banking with the dun tucked in close behind her. They rode through the water together, Shantih's high-stepping trot sending up a diamonded spray.

Shantih leapt up the opposite bank with ears pricked to follow the orange markers in another glorious gallop. But Jinny was ready for her, checked her back and holding her to a canter they rode on over the hillside.

The riders were fanned out now, some walking their horses downhill while a few had dismounted and were leading their mounts. One man on a black Fell pony was being carted off, his pony's head stuck between its knees. Knowing Bramble, Jinny felt a pang of sympathy. But there was no sign of Clare. She must have got well away.

According to Mike's watch they had been riding for over two hours when the route went through a gate and on to a road.

'You started after me,' a boy on a skewbald said to Jinny. 'I think you should slow down or you're going to be in too soon. And you want to calm her down or her heartbeat will be wild from the look of her.'

'It mostly *is* wild,' agreed Jinny, and they rode along together, chatting. Jinny thought how the whole ride had turned out like this, nothing to be afraid of. Although

106

there were to be placings nobody seemed too bothered, they were always ready to help each other.

As they walked along the day suddenly seemed to get colder, a dank, creeping cold and when Jinny glanced back she was amazed to see rolling mist blotting out the hills they had just ridden over.

The midway halt was in a field and as Jinny rode up it was already crowded with parked cars, back-up helpers, riders and horses. Miss Tuke was at the gate watching for Jinny.

'This way,' she said, hurrying Jinny and Shantih over to where Laura and her Mini were waiting. 'Down you come. I'll see to her. How's it going?'

'She was a bit wild to start with but super canters over the hills. Shantih loved it.'

Jinny swung her leg over Shantih's neck and slid to the ground. To her surprise her legs felt like chewed string. She made much of Shantih, clapping her and praising her, before Miss Tuke led her away.

'Food in the car,' said Laura, and Jinny was strangely quite ready to do what she was told; even willing to leave Shantih to Miss Tuke.

Sitting in the car Jinny gulped down orange juice and ate salad sandwiches. She lent her head on the back of the seat and was on the verge of sleep when Clare's voice blasted her awake.

'I'm frightfully pleased with him. Been going like a good 'un. It shows, breeding tells. No point in wasting time over some of these scrub beasts. It's the breeding that counts. There's a kid here with an Arab . . .'

'Shantih is a purebred Arab. I have her papers to prove it!' Jinny shouted, sticking her head out through the open car window.

Clare and the woman she had been talking to stared at Jinny as if she was some peculiar animal.

'Really,' said Clare. 'How fascinating,' and they walked away together totally ignoring Jinny.

'What an unfortunate girl,' said Laura and Miss Tuke returned, leading Shantih, to tell them that she had passed the vet without any trouble.

'Believe Gatsby just made it,' said Miss Tuke. 'His heartbeat was up. Far too heavy for this sort of thing, even a potter round like this.'

Out of the corner of her eye, Jinny saw Clare start off for the second part of the ride. She had another ten minutes to wait.

'I don't like the look of this mist,' said Miss Tuke, looking over the hills that were rapidly being swallowed up by the weaving skeins of mist.

'It can come down so quickly round here,' agreed Laura.

'Remember, keep to the markers,' Miss Tuke warned Jinny. 'Whatever you do don't stray off the route.'

Jinny was glad to be riding Shantih again. Knowing that Clare was only a few minutes in front of her spurred Jinny on. The mist dazzled her eyes, stinging in her nose and throat as she trotted on, keeping to the headland of a ploughed field. Two men who were riding just in front of Jinny held the gate open and they rode back on to a hill track. As the mist thickened the markers became more difficult to follow. Before, Jinny had been able to see the next marker and ride towards it but now she rode blindly between markers, seeing neither the next flag nor any other riders in front of her.

She passed one marker, its orange flag sodden in the mist, and rode on into the pearly whiteness wishing she had listened to Miss Tuke and put on the gloves she had offered her; feeling the edge of her crash helmet biting into the back of her neck. Shantih hated the mist. She trotted uneasily through it, spooking and shying.

108

'It's all right, there's nothing there. We can't crawl along like this or we're never going to beat Clare,' Jinny told her crossly.

The mist muffled Jinny's words; shrouded her in and suddenly she realized that there should have been another marker before this. She wondered if she had missed it or if a horse in front of her had kicked it aside. Jinny stopped, tried to peer into the mist but its flowing, diaphanous movement was as blinding as a wall. She rode on slowly, her eyes skinned for the next marker but there was none. In the distance she had ridden there should have been at least three more markers.

Jinny panicked, turned to ride back, then thought that was stupid. She should be galloping on, overtaking Clare, so she turned to ride on again and instantly had lost all sense of direction, was swallowed up by the mist.

'And whatever you do stay on the route,' warned Miss Tuke, her voice speaking in Jinny's mind.

Jinny shuddered. Standing still, she felt the dank chill of the mist settling into her bones; knew the fear of being lost and of having no idea what to do.

'Hey! Anyone there?' called a man's voice.

'Yes,' cried Jinny. 'Yes. Me,' and she rode Shantih towards the sound.

The two men who had been in front of her were as totally lost as Jinny. They rode on cautiously, just out of sight of each other, keeping contact with their voices, until one of the men found a marker.

'Flag!' he yelled, his voice jubilant.

'Well done,' said his companion. 'Now we keep together until we're out of this. The route goes up, along the crest of the hills after this, so I reckon we should ride out of it.'

'Should have cancelled it at the halfway halt when they

saw how thick the mist was,' said the first man. 'Too many novices riding to take any risks.'

They walked on together and then, almost from one stride to the next, they had ridden out of the mist into a world of brilliant blue sky and sun. The markers stretched out in front of them to the crest of the hills and the mist, beneath them now, was a vast sea of luminous cloud.

Jinny thanked the two men and they warned her to take care as she let Shantih canter. The route led along the very top of the rounded hills and Shantih, going at her smooth Arab canter, carried Jinny on.

They passed riders on tired horses – a few had dismounted and were leading their horses – but there was no sign of Clare.

'You don't need to get in before her. She started before you. All you need to do is finish the ride,' said the part of Jinny that was reasonable, easy going. 'But that wouldn't be enough, would it? You've got to pass her. Ride into the finish before her,' murmured the part of Jinny that whispered with a serpent's tongue.

Gradually the route sloped downwards. Jinny saw the dark rows of pine trees ahead. The mist was blowing about their branches, lying over the ground and breathing through the dark aisles between the trees.

Jinny rode into the forest alone. She had trotted Shantih down the hillside, unperturbed after Finmory's moors. Other riders were walking their horses cautiously, their faces absorbed in the effort of keeping their horses straight.

The route through the forest was along a broad ride, soft going with the ground churned by forestry machinery and poached by the horses that were in front of Jinny. The way was marked by orange tape circling the trunks of the pines.

The going was so deep that there was little Jinny could

110

do except walk – and Clare was still in front of her. Jinny, remembering from the plan that once you were through the forest you were back on the Country Club ground, pictured Clare riding triumphantly through the Finish.

'And sure to be placed,' Jinny thought bitterly.

At first the mist was only streamers winding through the trees, then a banking of white, swallowing up the lower branches, making Shantih wade knee deep through it. Then, without warning, the forest path dipped and they plunged into an under-mist world. But, for a second, just before the mists closed about her Jinny caught a glimpse of a rider on a heavy bay horse – a rider that could only be Clare.

Jinny pushed Shantih on, ignoring her as she stumbled through the mud.

'If we get level with her now,' Jinny told Shantih, 'we'll easily pass her on the run to the Finish. Tukey said Gatsby was done in after the first half so . . .'

The mist blotted out the trunks with their orange tape. But there was no way you could get lost in the forest, Jinny told herself. You only had to follow the track pitted with hoofprints. You could not go wrong.

Somewhere ahead of Jinny there was a crash and for a moment Jinny thought that they were cutting timber, then realized that was ridiculous, and decided that it must have been a dead branch falling. She rode Shantih on, thinking only of one thing – to beat Clare to the Finish.

A branch of a pine swept across Jinny's face; startling, icy cold, alien. Thinking she had wandered too far to one side of the track Jinny turned Shantih across to the other side. She had hardly taken two strides when the trees were beside her again.

Jinny pulled Shantih up. She couldn't think how the track had become so narrow. She couldn't have gone wrong for she was following hoofprints. Peering through the mist Jinny realized with biting dismay that she had been following only one set of hoofprints. Only one horse had ridden this way before her, perhaps a forest pony and not even someone from the ride.

'Blast it,' swore Jinny, swinging Shantih round to ride back the way she had come. At least this time she wasn't lost. She had only to pay attention to what she was doing and follow the hoofprints back to the right route.

The voice that shouted was a scream of pain and terror; a desperate demand for help. It was also, unmistakably, Clare Burnley's. It ripped through the mist like a gull's cry, searing Jinny's ears, making the hair rise on the back of her neck, her hands gather in Shantih's reins jabbing her to a halt, turning her to face in the direction of the screaming.

Clare must have taken the wrong track too. The hoofprints in front of Jinny must have been Gatsby's and Jinny wondered if the crash she had heard had been Gatsby as well.

The scream for help changed into a low, sobbing moan. Whatever had happened Clare had been badly hurt.

But Jinny did not ride to help her at once. She held Shantih in and through her mind spun all her reasons for hating Clare – her conceit and snobbishness; the way she had chased Shantih on to the moors when she could have kept her in one of her boxes until Jinny got home; the way she said Shantih was rubbish; her expensive horses that she brought up to Craigvaar so she would win at the local shows; the fact that her father was in charge of the demolition of the Wilton; and Jo Wilton dead.

Clare called again, her voice weaker. Yelling that she was coming, Jinny let Shantih plunge on towards the sound.

A little way ahead a forestry tractor was parked under the trees on the right of the track. On the left the muddy ground was churned with deep hoofprints and skid marks. A banking fell away from the track and at one place the brushwood and matting of dead branches were crushed and broken.

'Help! Help me!' and Clare's voice came from the mist at the bottom of the banking.

'I'm coming,' Jinny yelled. 'What's happened?'

She began to ride Shantih down the treacherous banking. Blowing through fearful nostrils Shantih picked her way down, hardly able to see more than a few steps in front of herself. They found themselves on a flat piece of ground littered with sawn-off branches and, although Clare had stopped shouting, Jinny could hear Gatsby's thrashing hooves. She rode towards the sound until on the other side of a four-barred fence she could just make out Gatsby's bulk stretched on the ground and Clare lying close to his head.

'Clare! Clare! It's Jinny. Are you all right?' and even though Jinny shouted at the pitch of her voice Clare continued to lie still. Only Gatsby struggled to get up. His hind legs seemed to be trapped and when he tried to haul himself up with his front legs his lashing hooves raked around Clare's head.

'Got to get to her,' Jinny thought desperately. 'Now, before Gatsby kicks her.

'It's a nothing fence,' Jinny told Shantih. 'You'll jump it easy.'

Had the fence been in a field Shantih would have cleared it easily but here, with no take-off, the ground deep in sawn-off branches, it was anything but a nothing fence. Yet Jinny did not think of leaving Shantih behind and climbing over by herself. That would have meant that Shantih would have been free to race back into the forest with all its dangers to a loose horse.

Gathering Shantih together, making absolutely certain

113

that Shantih knew she was going to be asked to jump, Jinny rode her at it. Just as Shantih was about to take off her front feet caught in a branch, entangling her and bringing her to her knees.

'Idiot,' Jinny told her, forcing herself to turn her nerves into fury not fear.

Jinny swung her round, and holding back her excited horse Jinny saw clearly in her mind Shantih blazing and brilliant lifting over the gate of her Glenbost field.

'When you can jump that you can hop over this,' and Jinny held the picture of Shantih jumping free in her mind as clearly as if she were going to paint it.

'Jump!' Jinny yelled. 'Jump it,' and she drove Shantih on. Taking off well before the fence Shantih sprang over the web of branches, leapt clear over and landed safely.

Praising her, Jinny slid to the ground and dashed to Clare. It looked as if Gatsby in his fright had jumped the fence, fallen on landing, throwing Clare off and trapping his back legs in a pit filled with lopped saplings. As Jinny approached he struggled again to free himself, his lashing front hooves narrowly missing Clare. Shouting at Gatsby, Jinny grabbed Clare under the arms and with all her strength dragged her away from Gatsby. Her face was putty yellow, her forehead gashed and covered in drying blood.

Jinny crouching beside her had no idea what to do. She could not leave her lying there while she tried to find help. Then she heard mist-muffled voices and hooves. She yelled at the top of her voice as the hoofbeats changing from a walk to a canter seemed to come from close below her. Shantih had heard them too. She stood listening intently as the sounds were lost in the mist.

'We must be at the very edge of the forest,' Jinny thought. 'The riders must be coming out of the trees and

114

cantering on down to the Club. If there were no mist I'll bet I could see it from here.'

Clare stirred, moaning to herself. She opened her eyes and saw Jinny.

'Where's Gatsby? Is he all right?' she asked and was unconscious again. Those were exactly the questions Jinny would have asked if she had had a fall on Shantih.

Forcing her mind away from the earth-shattering discovery that Clare Burnley was no different to herself Jinny tried to think of some way of getting help without leaving Clare lying there alone. Then the idea came to her.

She took off Shantih's tack, held her by her forelock and, when the next riders came cantering below them, Jinny released her.

'Go on,' she screamed. 'Go with them,' and she threw handfuls of leaf mould and pine cones at Shantih's quarters. The Arab paused, uncertain. 'Get on with you!' Jinny yelled, waving her arms wildly behind Shantih, and with a rattling whinny Shantih surged along a track and was swallowed by the mist.

'When she gets to the Club Miss Tuke will know there's something wrong. They'll send out search parties to look for us. It won't be long now,' Jinny told the unconscious Clare. She did not know what she could do to help her and she wasn't strong enough to try to free Gatsby by herself.

'If Petra was here, she'd know. She'd have her book,' Jinny thought wryly.

They came at last, shouting Jinny's name, blowing whistles, making enough noise to pierce the muffling mist. They disovered the place where Gatsby had refused to pass the tractor and plunged down the banking. They climbed down and heard Jinny's anxious shouts.

There were eight of them in the rescue party. Two

unrolled a stretcher, lifted Clare on to it and carried her down the way Shantih had taken. Three of the men managed to move the sawn-off saplings which had trapped Gatsby's hind legs and held his reins as he freed himself. He had a long tear down his off hind leg and was limping badly when they led him away. Jinny walked with the others back to the Club, asking about Shantih, making sure that she hadn't hurt herself; hearing how Miss Tuke had roused them up to send out a search party at once. Listening to them praising her – praising her for finding Clare when it had only been because she had taken the wrong route; praising her for sending Shantih for help when she hadn't thought of it, it had only been an idea that had come into her head. And talking about the mist, how next year they must have more mounted stewards.

When they reached the Club, riders were still coming through the Finish and being given their times – some grinning, some fighting back exhaustion and tears; each with their tales of adventures in the mist.

Jinny saw Miss Tuke's box and made her way slowly towards it. Seeing Shantih rugged and eating a feed Jinny knew she was safe.

'Dear horse,' she murmured, rubbing Shantih's neck. 'You are . . .' but feeling tears beginning to fill her eyes she went to perch on the side of the ramp, taking a mug of soup from Laura and telling Miss Tuke and Laura what had happened.

'Clare's been taken off to hospital,' Miss Tuke said. 'A doctor here saw her. He said the cut on her head isn't serious but she's concussed and has broken a leg. Gatsby's being stitched up. Quite a fall! It's after a smash like that that I know why I stick to trekking!'

Laura laughed but Jinny only clutched her hands closer round the comforting heat of her soup mug. Only she knew how close Clare had come to being killed by Gatsby's thrashing hooves.

And it had all been a nonsense – the way she had let herself hate Clare, her desperation to do better than Clare on the ride, when all the time there had been no one there to hate, only someone the same as herself who thought more of her horse than anything else.

Jinny stared at the bustle, the business of people and horses. All the people blinkered by the idea of doing well, doing better, doing best.

The Walker's voice in her mind was a windblown mist of sound.

'Choose. Choose the dance. Without you it is powerless.'

'Better get boxed up, then,' said Miss Tuke, slapping her thighs. 'Got to get back to my trekkers. Too much of this high living. Bit of a fiasco going home without a rosette. Still, it means we don't have to wait for the speeches.'

CHAPTER TWELVE

Jinny sat in the cabin of the box beside Miss Tuke, her heels caught on the edge of the seat, her arms wrapped round her knees. While Miss Tuke talked about treks and trekkers, Jinny stared through the windscreen reliving the ride; the warm feeling of togetherness when Shantih had given the dun pony a lead across the river; her fear when she had been lost in the mist before the two men found her; the glory of the high riding above the sunlit mist; Gatsby's hooves daggering into the ground within inches of Clare's face; and it not mattering that she had been disqualified for not completing the ride, not mattering at all. But beneath these thoughts whispered the voice of the Walker.

'Choose, choose the dance. It is powerless without you.'

'Early tomorrow I'll ride into Glenbost,' Jinny planned. 'The Bains go to Mass in Inverburgh every Sunday so I'll get a lift from them. I'll go straight to the Wilton, see the Horses,' and at the thought of seeing the Golden Horses again Jinny felt a tug at her heart, a longing, an ache of joy, like remembering Shantih when she woke in the morning. 'The men won't be working on a Sunday but I'll go all the same. And I'll dog off, spend all day Monday there.'

But the compulsion of the Walker's voice would not go away; was not satisfied.

Miss Tuke stood on her brakes making Shantih stagger and Jinny grab at the sides of the seat. The traffic lights for road works had turned to red.

'Thought I'd make it,' muttered Miss Tuke, drumming her stubby fingers impatiently on the wheel. 'Your typical Brit workman. Packs it in at Friday lunchtime, off to the pub and back on the job at the weekend for double time.'

Miss Tuke's words burst over Jinny like a north Atlantic breaker.

'Don't want Alice letting the trekkers near the ponies before I'm there to sort them out. Get their eye on a particular pony and that's it. Ride nothing else. Their pony! Huh! Happened before, you know. Had to trek all week with a never-seen-a-rocking-horse-in-her-life-before housewife, bonded on to the worst bolter I've ever had.'

The lights changed to orange and the horse box shot forward.

'Did you mean it?' demanded Jinny. 'That they stop on Friday and start again on Saturday?'

'All the time,' retorted Miss Tuke. 'Typical.'

And Jinny knew that she had to go to the Wilton now. Not tomorrow but now. She didn't know why, only that the Golden Horses needed her. As she had been needed to bring them from the cave so she was needed at this final destruction.

Now that there was no doubt left in Jinny the whispered intensity of the Walker had gone. She knew that she had to find a way to reach the Wilton and this knowing filled her with a new, vital energy. Nothing mattered except to reach the Wilton; to be there when its walls fell to the ground. If the demolition had been going on all day she might be too late. But Jinny didn't think so. She would still be in time if she went now.

'When do the trekkers usually arrive?' Jinny asked, manipulating her voice into genuine concern.

'Have to be there for tea. Usually all have it together. Lets me suss them out. Spot the thirty-four year olds that are over forty. The ladies that were nine stone when they filled in their application forms and have eaten themselves up to eleven stone since. Not going to make it today though,' and Miss Tuke, bent over the wheel, her eyes fixed on the horizon, foot flat down on the accelerator.

'If you dropped us at Glenbost . . .' Jinny began, knowing that there was no way in a million years that Miss Tuke would drive her to the Wilton.

'Wouldn't dream of it. I'll take you home,' but Miss Tuke's denial was not a hundred percent sure.

'I could easily lead Shantih home. I'm not a bit tired. And my book says that it's the best thing for a horse that has done a long ride, to be led about. Stops them stiffening up,' reasoned Jinny, picking at Miss Tuke's doubt.

'Wouldn't do her any harm,' admitted Miss Tuke.

'You would get back sooner.'

'Well . . .' said Miss Tuke. 'Would save a good bit of time, that's true.'

Head high, tail kinked and bannered over her back, Shantih sprang down the ramp and stood gazing expectantly towards Inverburgh as Jinny saddled her up.

'As if she knows,' thought Jinny, as Shantih whinnied wildly.

'Don't like dumping you like this,' said Miss Tuke, her mind already focused on her trekkers. 'Give me a phone.'

'It'll be good for Shantih,' repeated Jinny.

'She looks as if another ten-mile trek would be good for her,' said Miss Tuke, hauling up the ramp.

'Thank you,' said Jinny. 'Thank you for the day, for being back-up.'

'You're sure now?' said Miss Tuke, climbing into the cabin.

'Certain,' said Jinny, clutching Shantih's reins.

Miss Tuke started up the box. It trundled over the

120

rough ground, gathering power, turned in the direction of Ardtallon and was gone.

Jinny sprang into the saddle, felt Shantih full of going, prancing to be away. Jinny eased her reins and Shantih galloped forward.

As if the Red Sea drew back for them the traffic parted to let Jinny and Shantih through, or so it seemed to Jinny. 'And yet it can't possibly be like that,' she thought, as Shantih's reaching trot carried her towards Inverburgh and the Wilton. It was just chance that cars gave way to them, lorries slowed down and, as they reached Inverburgh, traffic lights changed to green at their approach. Just chance. Or was it? Perhaps this was how the magi had travelled, their minds so set on the purpose of their journey that lesser things ceased to exist.

Through the Inverburgh streets, crowded, jostling, frenetic with the beat of Saturday night they went. Yet Jinny was aware of nothing except the Wilton; to reach it before they tore down the Golden Horses; to see them for one last time. And just beyond the range of her hearing she was aware of the Walker calling them to him.

The evening was grey about them, the sun setting behind the city roofs as they reached the back streets that led to Carna Street. Suddenly Shantih whinnied and struck into a gallop, her hooves loud on the metalled road.

The thunderous noise of the JCB reverberated about them. They had reached the Wilton in the nick of time. A few people stood idly about. For a second they turned to stare curiously at Jinny and Shantih, but instantly their eyes were drawn back to the JCB as it rocked backwards and forwards over the rubble, waiting to destroy the Wilton.

Shantih stopped, stood alert and waiting, showing no

sign of nerves. She seemed unaware of the clang and rattle of the machinery and, even as the outside wall of the Wilton fell in crashing debris, she didn't move.

Jinny, too, sat motionless. She saw the wall fly open, heard the crashing roar of stone and saw the rising, blinding clouds of dust that billowed to their height then sank back to earth again.

Watching from a strange isolation, without thought or dread, she saw the JCB charge again a second time, against the inside wall of the Wilton. The bricks and plaster crumbled, and for minutes the dust blotted everything out. Then, as the setting sun fired the dust into a shimmering maze, her painting was exposed to the air. It was perfect, untouched by the carnage surrounding it.

'No,' cried Jinny. 'No,' but her voice made no sound.

She was torn by the waste, the futility – that the Horses should never dance again, for by this painting many people might have known the glory, the wholeness of the dance and been healed through it.

Jinny stared at the Golden Horses, absorbing them into herself. She did not see the JCB lumbering once more to the kill; was only aware of the moment before the wall fell apart. She could not bear it. She shouted 'No!' with her whole being; held the moment in the palm of her hand.

And in that moment the Horses lifted from the wall and danced. Bucking and rearing, they went running wild in an ecstacy of freedom through the sun-gilded maze of light. They rose in a spiralling dance, high above the dust of the Wilton, over the city roofs they went, galloping free, rising in light and joy.

'The best,' murmured Jo Wilton, who was himself again.

The wall roared down, settled into debris. The JCB rocked backwards and was still. The unsuspecting workman jumped down from the cabin and spoke to his mates. The few people who had been watching began to move away. It was over.

The Walker stood with his hand on Shantih's neck.

'If you had not come,' he said, 'they would have been lost forever. They could only find freedom through someone who had eyes to see them. Now they will always be here. Free from time or place. At all times, all places.'

The Walker's eyes held Jinny's. She saw the emerald green, the scarlet light in their dark depths. From a pocket in his black clothing the Walker took out a small parcel and handed it to Jinny. 'You have done well,' he said.

The sound of an urgent car's horn, men shouting, forced Jinny back into Carna Street's reality. She was blocking the road. Fumbling back into a world that for minutes seemed too small to contain her, Jinny rode Shantih to the side of the road and a van drove past. She put the parcel into her pocket, turned her attention to traffic and time. The few people who had been watching, realizing that the demolition was over, had begun to wander away. There was no sign of the Walker but the Wilton had been changed into fallen stone and rubble.

Still held by her vision of the dance, Jinny rode Shantih at a walk through Inverburgh, along the seemingly endless road to Glenbost and on to Finmory. As she rode she talked to Shantih, her voice speaking from her heart, saying things that she could never say to another human.

Mike had stuck a notice on the stable door saying he was leaving Bramble out for the night. Jinny checked Shantih over; watered and fed her but the Arab snatched her food down, ignored her hay and pushed at the box door wanting to be with Bramble.

So Jinny led her down to the field where Bramble was

waiting for her; watched while Shantih rolled, shook herself and settled to graze.

Jinny went quietly into the house through the front door. She could hear her family in the kitchen but she went on upstairs, climbing to her own room, closing the door behind her.

She stood in front of the Red Horse and opened the neat parcel that the Walker had left with her. Epona and the Horse god lay in her hands. Jinny gazed at them; conscious of the long years since their creation; conscious that she was holding them. Then she set them in front of the Red Horse and stood back, letting them go.

There was the sound of footsteps on the stairs, a touch on the door and Ken's voice saying, 'It's me.'

Jinny turned, taken by surprise as he came in; bright that it was not Mike or Petra; totally welcoming.

Ken saw the statues. Stood with Jinny and as they watched, the Red Horse, Epona and the Horse god seemed equal beings of power.

Through the open window they heard Shantih's clarion whinny ringing through the night and Jinny knew that the Walker was crossing over the Finmory moors, his work completed.

The Hardy Boys Mystery Stories

1	The Mystery of the Aztec Warrior	£2.25	☐
2	The Arctic Patrol Mystery	£2.25	☐
3	The Haunted Fort	£2.25	☐
4	The Mystery of the Whale Tattoo	£2.25	☐
5	The Mystery of the Disappearing Floor	£2.25	☐
6	The Mystery of the Desert Giant	£2.25	☐
7	The Mystery of the Melted Coins	£2.25	☐
8	The Mystery of the Spiral Bridge	£2.25	☐
9	The Clue of the Screeching Owl	£2.25	☐
10	While the Clock Ticked	£2.25	☐
11	The Twisted Claw	£2.25	☐
12	The Wailing Siren Mystery	£2.25	☐
14	The Secret of Pirate's Hill	£2.25	☐
16	The Secret of the Old Mill	£2.25	☐
21	What Happened at Midnight	£2.25	☐
22	The Sinister Signpost	£2.25	☐
41	The Mysterious Caravan	£2.25	☐
42	Danger on Vampire Trail	£2.25	☐
43	The Bombay Boomerang	£2.25	☐
44	The Masked Monkey	£2.25	☐
45	The Shattered Helmet	£2.25	☐
46	The Clue of the Hissing Serpent	£2.25	☐

ARMADA

POLICE FILES

EVER THOUGHT YOU'D MAKE A GOOD DETECTIVE? WELL HERE'S YOUR CHANCE TO PROVE IT.

Question suspects
Interview witnesses
Search for fingerprints
Conduct lab. tests
Consult the police computer

To solve each of the four crimes you must piece together all the evidence taken both from individual case files and the material held on the police computer. Only by careful deduction will you be able to catch the criminals. All the information is hee – but like any good detective, you have to know the right questions to ask . . .

A game for one or more players.

£2.95 ☐

ARMADA

All these books are available at your local bookshop or newsagent, or can be ordered from the publisher. To order direct from the publishers just tick the title you want and fill in the form below:

Name _____

Address _____

_____

Send to: Collins Childrens Cash Sales
PO Box 11
Falmouth
Cornwall
TR10 9EN

Please enclose a cheque or postal order or debit my Visa/ Access –

Credit card no:

Expiry date:

Signature:

– to the value of the cover price plus:

UK: 60p for the first book, 25p for the second book, plus 15p per copy for each additional book ordered to a maximum charge of £1.90.

BFPO: 60p for the first book, 25p for the second book plus 15p per copy for the next 7 books, thereafter 9p per book.

Overseas and Eire: £1.25 for the first book, 75p for the second book. Thereafter 28p per book.

ARMADA